THE DARK COTTAGE

Half past five. Where on earth was her friend James? What they needed now was to get away from this God-forsaken cottage at Forest Brook and find somewhere that served tea. Somewhere commonplace and comforting that belonged to the ordinary everyday world.

Where was James? Was he trying to break into the house again? Had he succeeded?

Suddenly Paula was struck with a notion that made her jump out of the yellow mini and run towards the house. Why had they both been so sure the house was empty? The bell had not been answered, but that meant nothing. The letter taped to the front door had been intended to drive them away. Or had it? Had it been intended to arouse their curiosity? After all, they had broken in once: why not again?

Was someone waiting silently inside all this time to see whether the bait had worked? In other words, had she and James walked into a trap?

ANNA CLARKE

THE MYSTERY LADY

CHARTER BOOKS, NEW YORK

This Charter book contains the complete
text of the original edition.
It has been completely reset in a typeface
designed for easy reading, and was printed
from new film.

THE MYSTERY LADY

A Charter Book / published by arrangement with
Doubleday, a division of Bantam Doubleday Dell
Publishing Group, Inc.

PRINTING HISTORY
Doubleday edition published 1986
Charter edition / December 1989

Charter Books are published by The Berkley Publishing Group,
200 Madison Avenue, New York, New York 10016.
The name "CHARTER" and the "C" logo
are trademarks belonging to Charter Communications, Inc.

PRINTED IN THE UNITED STATES OF AMERICA

10 9 8 7 6 5 4 3 2 1

---— *1* —---

The restaurant was a few minutes' walk from Piccadilly Circus. It was a sombre place, with its dark-brown paintwork and olive-green chairs, but it was quiet and there was plenty of space between the tables. It was also very expensive, and it was patronized by those who wished to speak and be heard rather than those who wished only to see and be seen.

At a table by the window, where the gloom of the room was brightened by the colours of the petunias massed in the window-box, two people sat studying their menus. One of them was a big man in his early seventies, chubby-faced, almost bald, and giving a first impression of benevolence that was belied if one looked more closely at the icy-blue eyes.

This was George Bruce, head of a very successful publishing business and the despair of rival publishers, who longed for him to retire and leave the firm to a more orthodox and less aggressive management.

His companion was a slight, fair woman in her late thirties, wearing a plain blue cotton dress, no jewellery, and little make-up. She looked rather severe while she was reading, but as soon as she spoke, or was spoken to, the neat, regular features were filled with an eagerness and a vitality that gave them beauty.

The middle-aged waitress who was taking their orders could tell that the woman at the table was nervous. Her right hand kept pushing at her hair, which had started off, after a visit to the ladies' room, as a glossy corn-coloured bell, but was

1

quickly becoming more and more untidy. This, decided the waitress, was probably its normal condition.

She looked clever, though. And also quite unselfconscious. An author, obviously, but neither one of the top sellers nor one of the very new ones, overawed and desperately anxious to make a good impression.

Mr. Bruce ordered soup, as he always did. The woman opposite him asked for the same, but the waitress could tell that she really wanted it and was not just following his lead. She asked for roast duckling to follow, while Mr. Bruce wanted his usual steak.

The waitress departed. Her judgment was quite correct. Mr. Bruce's companion was Paula Glenning, Ph.D., author of a somewhat offbeat biography of the famous contemporary novelist G. E. Goff, which dealt less with the great man's own work than with the way in which that work had affected his two wives and his household. It was a scholarly piece of work which could, if rightly handled, also have quite wide popular appeal.

"Here's to *Shadowed Lives*," said George Bruce, raising his glass. "We're getting good press coverage, and it will receive approximately seven minutes of radio time in 'Books of Today' this evening."

"You never told me," said Paula, looking up at the publisher reproachfully.

"It was only fixed up this morning. They always do these things at the last minute."

"And who will be talking about my book?"

"Richard Grieve, of course." The big man beamed at her. "The greatest authority on G. E. Goff. Personally, I can't see why anybody should be content to make their own name by becoming an authority on another man, but that's what you literary folk seem to do. He will sell it to all the highbrows, and we'll have to think of other ways to reach the lesser mortals."

"Richard never told me," said Paula in a rather hurt voice as the waitress removed the plates.

George Bruce raised one eyebrow. "Friend of yours?"

"Richard and I used to be good friends," replied Paula, but did not add that it had never been quite the same since she told him that she could not marry him. Richard was a vulnerable and sensitive person under the rather formidable public persona of scholar and critic, and indiscreet though Paula sometimes was, she was certainly not going to talk about him to George Bruce, who was a notorious gossip.

In fact, Paula was almost beginning to wish that she had never offered the book to George Bruce at all. She ought now to be drinking a meagre glass of sherry in the austere surroundings of a university press to celebrate its publication, instead of sitting opposite this flamboyant personage in this very exclusive restaurant. It was James Goff, grandson of the subject of the book, who taught English Literature in the same London college as she taught herself, who had suggested George.

Paula had been doubtful. Surely Bruce only published thrillers and romances and sensational stuff. He wouldn't be interested in an academic study with little general appeal. James had replied that he understood that George Bruce was trying to get into the academic field and wipe out completely the faint aura of disreputability that still hung about the firm. In the early years, just after the war, they had been notorious for printing the sort of thing that others were afraid to touch for fear of the laws of obscenity and blasphemy that were still in force at the time. It was all quite different now, said James. The firm was very respectable indeed; or else everybody else had sunk down to the same level, take it which way you wanted.

Gratitude to James for his generous help with her researches, combined with Paula's own impulsiveness, drove her to write the letter that had set in motion a process that was gratifying in many ways, but that was also beginning to alarm her.

"You'll do fine on the telly chat shows," George was saying. "Nice to look at but not too glamorous. Friendly but not assertive. Straightforward. Unaffected."

"I've never been on television," said Paula faintly.

"Well, you're going now. You don't seem to realize, young woman, that you've got a winner in that book of yours. Famous English novelist—they all know the name even if they've never read a word of his—the women in his life, unhappy marriage, divorce, mysterious second wife, dramatic death. Touch of feminism but not too much. Sympathy for the downtrodden. Just you go on being yourself and the sales of *Shadowed Lives* will take care of themselves. But that wasn't what I wanted to talk about today,'' he went on, overriding Paula's increasingly vigorous protests. ''I want to talk about your next book.''

''My next book, if it ever appears,'' said Paula, making herself heard at last, ''will be a collection of essays on modern American poets.''

This remark produced a silence. Paula occupied herself with her portion of duckling, feeling that she had won a little respite. George, slicing at his steak with quick, impatient gestures, was wondering how best to proceed. It was his firmly held belief, which up till now had been very little challenged, that nobody was immune to flattery in some form or another and that everybody had his or her price. The author of *Shadowed Lives* was an intelligent and honest woman who seemed to have few illusions about herself, but she was certainly no exception to the general rule. How could he advance his project in a way that would appeal to her without letting her suspect for a moment that he had a twofold motive for suggesting that she should undertake research for this particular book?

He had no doubt that she was the right person. The idea had come into his head when he first read the manuscript of *Shadowed Lives*, and had grown stronger and stronger as he came to know her personally. Inquisitive and persistent, with impeccable professional credentials, and with an open and friendly manner that made people warm to her and inspired confidence. She had made an excellent job of G. E. Goff, and in order to be a good biographer one must be a good detective. That was another of his firmly held beliefs. It was a detective that he wanted, but Paula Glenning must think he only wanted a biographer.

''I've been wanting for some time,'' he said at last, ''to publish a book about Rosie O'Grady. No, not the lady in the song, but the author. But I've never been able to find the right sort of person to write it. I have found her now.''

And he raised his glass to Paula, who was unable to conceal her astonishment.

''Rosie O'Grady the Mystery Lady?'' she said. ''The author of over fifty romantic adventure stories, who is herself the greatest mystery of all? You've never got *her* to appear on television chat shows,'' she concluded with a hint of asperity.

"I've never tried," said George. "That would spoil the whole image. There's two ways of attracting attention. One is to show everything and the other is to show nothing. Combine the two and you have—"

"Strip-tease," interrupted Paula, beginning to laugh.

"Exactly. We've had a long run of the mysterious best-selling writer and it's time for the real Rosie O'Grady to be exposed to view. She's getting old now and I've got a nasty suspicion that she's written herself out. We've got a couple of manuscripts held in reserve, and after that I'd like to bring out the Rosie O'Grady Story, by Paula Glenning, author of *Shadowed Lives*. We'll call it *The Heart of the Mystery*, and it's up to you to make sure that there's something there and not just an empty shell. There'll be a lot of research to do and you like research, don't you," went on George as he refilled Paula's glass. "It needs a scholar," he added as Paula still made no response. "A scholar with imagination as well as an inquiring mind. A sympathetic person with a genuine interest in people and what makes them tick. It's going to be a sensation, this life story." Once again he raised his glass. "Rosie O'Grady the Mystery Lady," he said solemnly. "The puzzle is solved at last. By Paula Glenning."

"But I haven't got time," said Paula feebly. "I have a full-time job teaching college students."

"You're not going to need that anymore when the royalties start rolling in. Or even when you get your advance, come to that."

"But I like teaching. It's my life."

"You also like nosing into other people's lives, don't you?"

"I suppose so," agreed Paula unhappily.

"And there's plenty of others I've got in mind when you've finished with Rosie."

Paula pushed aside her plate. Her normally healthy appetite had deserted her. George Bruce's preposterous suggestion was beginning to look less impossible every minute. But it would turn her whole life upside down, the safe, reliable, and on the whole gratifying life of a university lecturer that she had achieved for herself after a lot of hard work and that had kept her afloat through all her own times of personal crisis.

"Literary detective stories," said George, ignoring her agitation. "There are great possibilities of an expanding market there. I definitely want the O'Grady book, but after that you can choose for yourself."

The waitress handed Paula a menu and she stared at it without seeing a word. "Oh. Just coffee, please," she said at last.

"In a couple of weeks' time the long summer vacation will begin," said George. "That will give you three months clear."

"But I'm working on my modern American poets."

"Have you got a contract for it?"

"Not exactly," said Paula reluctantly.

"Then they can go in the freezer. O'Grady can't wait. According to her agent, the old girl's had several heart attacks already. And then there's that faithful old retainer of hers, Robin Key, who's looked after her household and all her business affairs for ever. You want to talk to him quick, before he goes gaga or pops off himself."

"Who is Robin Key?" asked Paula, interested in spite of her resolution to decline George's offer. "A sort of secretary?"

"Heaven alone knows. We only know that he handles everything—correspondence, contracts, revisions to manuscripts, money."

"You've never seen Rosie, then?"

"Only once. She came to the office about six years ago."

"And what did she look like?"

Paula knew now that she was lost, sinking ever deeper into her own well of curiosity about the Mystery Lady.

"Tall, gaunt, grey," replied George. "Dripping with furs. It was that very cold winter. Can you imagine Virginia Woolf grown old and smothered in make-up and soaked in perfume? Well, that was Rosie. Rather revolting really. She didn't stay long and didn't say much. She'd got a cold, too. Sounded very hoarse and was sucking some ghastly menthol lozenges. I had to leave my office for the next couple of hours while my secretary aired the room and got the smell out."

Paula was listening avidly.

"She said she was very pleased with the way we were handling her books," continued George, "and that she was thinking of writing a play. I'd hoped to get a photograph—all we'd ever had was that dim profile that we used to put on the book jackets, but as soon as I saw her, I decided against it. Let the mystery remain. The reality was best kept secret.''

''Then why do you want to open it up now?''

''Because, my dear Paula, I believe she is failing fast. Our editors have had to do a lot of work on the last two manuscripts, and even then, it's only the name that's selling them. By any other author, they'd have gone straight into the slush heap.''

''Poor Rosie,'' said Paula.

''Rich Rosie,'' countered George. ''Very rich Rosie indeed. And don't you dare come at me with your 'money isn't everything' because I know it isn't, but the things that money can't buy can still be exploited to make money. Love, honour, sacrifice, and all the rest of it. They're the very stuff of fiction, and fiction is something that people are prepared to pay an awful lot of money for. Fiction is essential for the survival of the human race. Truth is not.''

Paula, whose mind had begun to seethe with refutations of this provocative statement, was too slow in coming forward with them. George continued to enjoy himself on what was obviously one of his favourite themes.

''Truth, if it exists, is the last thing people need,'' he went on, ''and they'll slither away from it or gloss it over immediately it rears its head. Look at the great religions of the world. Revelations of truth? Maybe they are, but how long do they last before turning into myths and stories? Gospel stories, Buddha stories, rabbi stories. That's what rules people's lives. Fictions, not truths.''

''Are you trying to tell me,'' said Paula, who had decided that it was pointless to argue, ''that it doesn't matter whether I discover the truth about Rosie O'Grady and that I can just make the whole thing up?''

''You wouldn't be able to,'' retorted George. ''You've spent too long in the academic world. It's death to the imagination, this constant fussing around with so-called facts. If you can find any facts, then treat 'em as a starting point, not a conclusion. You'll have to go down to Sussex and talk to Robin Key and anybody else you can find. You might even get to see Rosie herself. Depends if she's really ill or not. But if so, then there'll be a doctor. Nurses, maybe. And you'd better drop in and see her agent before you go. It's Willie Broadway. I doubt whether he knows any more than I do, but one can't be sure. He may have one or two leads that you could follow. We'll go back to the office now and I'll get my secretary to write letters of introduction."

"But I don't even know that I want the job," cried Paula desperately as they got up from the table.

George Bruce was greeting acquaintances at neighbouring tables and appeared not to hear her.

They came out into bright sunlight in Piccadilly and were too engulfed by crowds to be able to talk. In the quieter side street, Paula said, "Look, it sounds fascinating and it's terribly tempting and I've no objection to earning a lot of money, but all the same I don't want to do this book. I can't do it. It's outside my range."

George Bruce stood still and looked down at her. Paula braced herself for another onslaught, but when he spoke his voice was quiet and kindly.

"I think you underestimate yourself. It's a great pity."

Twenty minutes later she was getting into a taxi, burdened with a large envelope that contained a lot of O'Grady novels in paperback, some photocopies of correspondence, and letters of introduction to William Broadway and to Robin Key.

In the traffic snarl-up in Regent Street, Paula stared out of the taxi and envied the people who were jostling on the sidewalks or looking longingly at the window displays in Burberrys and Libertys. She would have given anything to be out among those tourist crowds, gazing at clothes that she could never afford to buy, and looking forward to a pleasant summer vacation driving around Brittany with her sister and family before settling down to work in the British Museum Library.

Whatever George Bruce might say, the academic life suited her. It was at the same time structured and unconstricted, and for somebody who, like herself, seemed incapable of a lasting marriage or other personal relationship, it provided plenty of variety and human interest. She ought to have stuck to her own life-style instead of breaking away into the sort of biography that had led her into publicity interviews that scared her, and was now leading her into an even more alarming unknown.

"Mr. Robin Key, High Beechwoods, near Forest Brook, Sussex."

It sounded like one of those remote rural spots where the nearest public transport was one bus a week from the village six miles away. Paula had no car, and George Bruce had told her to take taxis to everything and charge it to expenses, but it went against her thrifty upbringing; and besides, the more she spent on this crazy enterprise, the more would she feel obliged to deliver the goods. And how was she going to do that when all she would find at High Beechwoods was a sick old woman who refused to see her and a surly old bodyguard who refused to talk?

The taxi seemed to be now permanently stationed opposite the window of a newly opened shoe shop in Oxford Street. Paula was fascinated by some red-and-gold sandals, and craned forward to read the price tag. It looked like sixty pounds. Not my scene, she told herself as the taxi moved on at last. But when they drew up at the row of high Victorian terrace houses in the shabbier part of Hampstead, she thought: Perhaps it could be my scene if George Bruce is right. The prospect was alarming. Maybe Rosie O'Grady lived like a recluse in order to avoid having to deal with her publisher.

Paula climbed the three flights of stairs to her attic apartment and was immediately comforted by the sight of the overflowing bookshelves and the litter of papers on the desk. This was her refuge and her domain and she was never going to change it. If she took on the O'Grady job, it would not be for the money, but out of sheer curiosity. George Bruce was right about that. The mystery of other people's lives was an irresistible temptation to her.

2

William Broadway, literary agent, was a weary-looking elderly man who sat behind an incongruously large desk and looked at the papers in front of him and not at Paula when he spoke.

"After the war, 1949. That's when we received the first O'Grady manuscript. My father dealt with it. I'd only joined the firm recently. It was badly written and badly typed and needed a lot of editing before it was fit to send to a publisher. All the O'Grady novels have required substantial revision, but fortunately that became George Bruce's worry, not ours. He didn't like our editors, and preferred to arrange for the work himself."

"Why did you take her on then?" asked Paula. "Her work seems to have been unsatisfactory."

"We believed that she had the vital spark, and we have not been proved wrong. Here is the covering letter that came with the first typescript."

Paula received a small piece of pale-blue paper, yellowing round the edges, covered with backward-sloping handwriting.

"Please find enclosed a tale of mystery and romance," she read. "Please find a publisher for it and let me know how much they are going to pay. Yours very truly, R. O'Grady."

The address at the top was "2, Railway Cottages, Brighton, Sussex," and there was a postscript that read: "My book is called 'The Courage of Caroline.' "

Paula repeated this title inquiringly.

"It had to be changed," said Mr. Broadway. "Even for those days it sounded too much like a girls' school story. Half a dozen publishers turned it down and George Bruce finally printed it under the title *The Haunted House Mystery*."

"I prefer 'The Courage of Caroline,' " said Paula.

William Broadway sighed. "Yes. Schoolgirl stories have become acceptable again. It's all a matter of fashion, of going with the trend."

He looked and sounded more tired than ever.

"I'm taking up your time," said Paula. "Would it be possible for me to have a look at the O'Grady files? I don't mean removing them from the office, but George Bruce did say . . ."

"My secretary will find you a desk," said the literary agent. "If there's anything you need to ask me, you must let me know."

Paula was relieved to get away from the gloomy room and to sit at a small table in a crowded office with a cheerful middle-aged woman who introduced herself as Frances Merivale.

"Don't take any notice of Willie," she said. "He fancies himself as a poet and he never wanted to come into the business at all and he's terribly jealous of George Bruce. He ought to have thought of the O'Grady Story himself and he didn't."

"Did you ever see her?" asked Paula after she had been making notes for some time.

"Only once," replied Frances, and described Rosie in much the same terms as George had done, but added that she had felt rather sorry for her, because she really had seemed rather an unattractive personality, who appeared to be deriving very little pleasure from all her wealth and fame. "I wondered whether that was the secret of her success," she concluded. "That the novels were day-dreams, making up for the excitement and romance that she'd never known in her own life. You get that sometimes with romantic novelists."

"But how do you know that she never had any excitement or romance?" said Paula, turning over papers in the file. "Nobody seems to know anything about her own life at all. There's only this tiny biographical note. 'Born in Canada in 1905; went to school there; apprenticed to a milliner and

worked in the hat trade. Now lives in Sussex, England.' Is
that all you've got?''

"It's all we've ever had," said Frances Merivale. "Most
people write reams on their biographical forms. Apparently
they had great difficulty getting even this much out of Rosie.''

"Perhaps she doesn't exist," said Paula. "Maybe she's
some terribly highbrow novelist leading a double life.''

"I believe that was Mr. Bruce's theory at one time, and
that he actually had somebody do a bit of detective work,
who came to the conclusion that Rosie O'Grady was a real
person. Didn't he tell you about it?''

"No," said Paula thoughtfully. "I wonder why.''

"He'd rather you came to your own conclusions, I suppose," said Frances, and looked as if she would like to continue on this theme, but the telephone rang and as she
appeared to be caught up in some lengthy business, Paula
took her leave and was invited to come in again whenever
she wanted.

The office was in Jermyn Street, and Paula walked slowly
towards Trafalgar Square, feeling rather disappointed. Who
was going to help her in these researches if not the agent and
the publisher who stood to gain from them? But the former
appeared completely uninterested, and as for George, had he
not himself proclaimed that fiction was more important than
truth? No doubt he lived up to his beliefs, and one could not
trust him at all.

Paula arrived at the bus stop to see the number 159 that
would take her to Hampstead pulling away. This seemed to
be a day for little frustrations. Impatient to be doing something, she got onto the number 77 instead, which would take
her near the college, where she would collect her mail.

At the main entrance she ran into James Goff, who was in
less of a hurry than usual, and inclined to be chatty.

"How's the book going?" he asked.

"Hopeless. I don't know how I'm ever going to get
started," she replied.

"What on earth are you talking about, Paula?" asked
James. "*Shadowed Lives* was published last month, wasn't
it? Oh, for God's sake, let's get out of this place," he went
on impatiently, pulling her down the steps after him. "There's
a vacation course going on here that seems to consist entirely

of Japanese computer experts and they're making me feel as if I'm the one who is the visitor from outer space. I've got the car here. Let's get out of London. Where shall we go?"

"Brighton," said Paula, suddenly inspired.

James groaned. "It'll be just as bad. I mean somewhere peaceful."

"Brighton," repeated Paula firmly.

On the way she told him about the Rosie O'Grady book. George Bruce had strongly hinted that he didn't want it talked about just yet, and Paula knew well that James, in addition to being rather indiscreet, was not above making use of other people's ideas; but she was becoming so depressed about the whole project that she was past caring. She had signed a contract and received a large advance on royalties, which made her more nervous than ever.

James listened with great interest. He was an erratic driver at the best of times, and their progress through the southern suburbs of London was nerve-racking. By the time they were halfway to the coast, Paula had acquired a headache and insisted on stopping for tea. In a cool hotel lounge, low-ceilinged and oak-beamed, with leaded windows overlooking a lawn and rambler roses, Paula recovered and smiled at him affectionately. They had once been lovers and had graduated to friendship, an exceptionally comfortable and relaxed and undemanding friendship.

"I'm dreading the visit to High Beechwoods," confessed Paula. "Mr. Robin Key sounds unwelcoming, to put it mildly."

"I'll come with you," said James. "You'll need transport in any case, and I can pick up the pieces if he chucks you out."

"But we may need several visits," objected Paula. "I thought you were going to China with the Wong woman this summer."

"It's all off," said James abruptly.

Paula maintained a sympathetic silence. James had been notorious in the past for the number and variety of his girl-friends, but he was no longer a young man, and it rather looked as if the time was coming when his selfishness sometimes outweighed his charms.

An Indian girl in an emerald-green sari came to take their

order. She was courteous and efficient and looked very exotic in the rural English surroundings.

"Ye Olde English Tea Shoppe has gone the way of everything else," said James sadly. "Soon there'll be nothing English left except over-cooked cabbage and inadequate plumbing. We're getting old, Paula."

"Forty," she replied briskly. "The prime of life."

"But I haven't achieved anything. I've nothing to show for it. I've just frittered along."

"You had the great disadvantage of being a spoilt only child and always having too much money. In the circumstances it's been quite an achievement to stick to a job at all. And to do it well," she added. James Goff was a careless and slapdash scholar but a surprisingly good teacher.

The tea and cakes were excellent, and James gradually cheered up.

"Shall we go to High Beechwoods straight away?" he suggested as he studied the road map. "It's only about thirty miles from here."

Paula was tempted. "Except that they probably won't even let us in without an appointment."

"We could snoop around. Chat to the neighbours."

"I don't think they've got any neighbours. No, let's stick to the chronological order. Rosie was first heard of from Railway Cottages in Brighton."

"They'll have been pulled down long ago and replaced by high-rise housing estates."

"Very likely. If so, we go on to Forest Brook."

But they found the Cottages at last, after many inquiries and many false turnings, alongside a disused railway terminal not very far from the sea front. All around were demolition works, and the area was obviously being cleared for development.

"We're only just in time," said James, looking at the row of little flint-faced houses standing lonely among the dirt and the debris. "They're mostly boarded up and unoccupied."

"It's a pity," said Paula, stopping in front of number 4 to admire the front garden, which was bright with petunias and nasturtiums. "They could be charming."

"Probably full of dry rot and haven't got bathrooms," said

James. "Hi—we're in luck. Number 2 has someone living there."

Paula felt a little stirring of excitement. The quest for Rosie O'Grady had come alive again. They were on the trail.

"I'll wait in the car," said James. "I don't want to butt in."

But he was obviously longing to be with her.

"Come on," said Paula. "This is a joint venture. If the book ever gets written, we'll be co-authors, and George Bruce can take it or leave it."

As they pushed open the low wooden gate they could sense the eyes looking at them from the neighbouring windows. Apart from a battered Ford van, James's Rover was the only vehicle standing in the dusty roadway. No attempt had been made to make a garden at number 2 Railway Cottages. An untrimmed privet hedge straggled over the wooden fencing, and the rough grass was strewn with bits of old piping, rusty iron, and an ancient kitchen sink.

A young man in jeans and a T-shirt opened the door just as James and Paula reached it.

"Not for sale," he said abruptly before they could speak. "We're being demolished. Can't you see?"

"Well, actually we were thinking of buying an old cottage in Brighton and doing it up," said Paula, "and we thought we'd look around before going to the estate agents, but if these are going to be pulled down . . ."

She glanced at James. The young man looked the sort who would prefer not to do business with a woman.

"Are there any similar terraces in the neighbourhood?" asked James, taking his cue. "I don't want to delay you, I can see you're busy, but if you happened to know of any—"

"You'd better ask the wife," was the slightly more amiable reply. "She's always ready for a chat." And he jerked his head over his shoulder towards the front door and went off down the garden path and got into the Ford van.

"We'll talk about cottages and then I'll try to bring in Rosie," whispered Paula to James.

The young woman who came down the stairs to greet them was thin and dark and seemed very agitated. She barely gave them a chance to put their question, but poured out a stream of complaints about Railway Cottages—drains always getting blocked up, walls so thick you couldn't knock a nail in, and then all the demolition work, the dust and the dirt and the noise—no wonder she had these headaches and had to take tablets for her nerves. And Morris had been in a bad temper all the time they'd been living here because he'd been promised a council flat and they'd put someone in ahead of them, but now they were moving at last, next week, to the new estate at Elmdean.

"I hope you'll be very happy there," said James when she paused at last for breath. "But I expect the old people will be sorry to go."

This produced a fresh flood. Mrs. Martyr, at number 4, had apparently refused to be rehoused. She had sworn that nothing on earth would ever move her. Bulldozers and local authorities might do their worst. She had been born in number 4 Railway Cottages and lived there all her life, and that was where she was going to die.

"She's off her nut," added the girl. "Morris swears she's got a gun and it'll end up in a siege and a shoot-out."

The prospect of such drama seemed to cheer her up a little. James and Paula exchanged glances.

"We mustn't keep you any longer," said Paula. "Thanks for giving us the address of the estate agent."

They got away at last.

"Number 4," said James as they reached the roadway.

Paula nodded. "But I only hope she doesn't think we've come from the Town Hall."

"And produce that gun?"

They smiled at each other. It was good to have company, thought Paula. James's optimism was just what she needed, and she began to feel that she might really be on the trail of Rosie O'Grady at last.

The net curtains in the front window of number 4 shifted slightly as they walked up the garden path. Paula dawdled, admiring the flowers.

"Hollyhocks," she said. "My grandmother used to love them."

"That's right," said James. "Put yourself into the nostalgic mood."

He touched the brass door knocker. It was in the form of

a ship's anchor, very bright and shining, and the green paint on the door was equally clean.

"She must be scrubbing away all the time," murmured Paula, "with all this dust around. I wish she'd hurry up. I'm getting nervous."

They put their heads close to the door and could hear mouselike scrabblings behind it.

"She's probably barricaded herself in," said James, "and is having to shift the sideboard."

"Ssh," warned Paula.

"Who are you?" came a cracked old voice, sounding eerily close to them. "What do you want?"

"We want to talk about Rosie O'Grady," said Paula.

"What's that? Can't hear you."

"We want to ask you about Rosie O'Grady." Paula's voice was now loud and clear. By this time all the remaining inhabitants of Railway Cottages, including Morris, who had come back in his van, were listening and watching with great interest.

"You sound like the police," murmured James, "come to ask what she has done with the body."

Paula began to laugh. "Well, we are sort of detectives."

The door was opened at last and they squeezed through with difficulty. The dark little hall was crowded with sharp-edged pieces of furniture.

"In here," said the voice, and they manoeuvered themselves into the kitchen, which made Paula exclaim aloud in delight because it was so much like an illustration from a Beatrix Potter story, with its scrubbed wooden dresser and the willow-pattern plates, and the black cooking-range with the iron kettle, and the rag rugs on the stone floor.

And Mrs. Martyr herself fitted perfectly into the picture. She was small and wiry and wore a blue-and-white-striped apron and her fluffy white hair was scraped up into a bun on the top of her head above her sunburnt face and her very shrewd dark eyes.

"Sit down," she commanded, and waited for them to settle themselves into the two Windsor chairs before she went on: "Who are you and what's all this about Rosie O'Grady?"

3

As James said to Paula later, if any of those publishing people had really wanted to know Rosie's history, they could have taken the trouble to visit Railway Cottages themselves. But they would have got nothing out of Mrs. Martyr, retorted Paula, because they would not have known how to approach her.

James Goff knew exactly how to approach her. He could be as charming with old ladies as he was with young, and to Mrs. Martyr, who really did seem to be very old indeed, he was still, though forty, a good-looking young man.

"We want to know something about Rosie O'Grady because we like her books so much, my friend and I," he said. "Do you read much yourself?"

Mrs. Martyr's bright brown eyes surveyed first James and then Paula. "Friends," she said. "Just good friends." And she clasped her knotted hands together and leaned forward, shaking with laughter.

When she had finished, James put the question in a different way. "I don't suppose you've got much time to read novels yourself," he added.

"I read plenty of novels, young man," she replied, "and I know the books you mean and I think they're rubbish, every one of them. And I can tell you this much more. Whoever the author is, she isn't my Rosie O'Grady. My Rosie O'Grady never wrote a story in her life. Hardly could write at all, poor thing, so my mother used to say. I didn't know about it myself. She seemed very grown-up to me, being ten years older

18

than me, and that's a lot when you're only six. Six I was
when she went away. Or it might have been seven.''

Paula longed to look at James, but dared not to do so.
Mrs. Martyr, apparently sunk in the past, was nevertheless
watching their every movement, and watching for the effect
of her words. Paula sat as still as she could and did her utmost
to appear both interested and neutral. Any talking to be done
was obviously best left to James.

''She went away, did she,'' he murmured, giving his whole
attention to the old lady and refraining from glancing at Paula.

''To foreign parts,'' said Mrs. Martyr. ''Broke her poor
mother's heart. And my mother's too. They were like that''—
and she unclasped her hands and hooked the two forefingers
together—''Rosie's mother and mine. Neighbours all their
lives. No, not exactly neighbours, because there's number 3
in between, but number 3 has always been an unlucky house.
Nobody ever stops there for long.''

She paused and seemed for a moment to be quite with-
drawn from them, looking inward at her memories.

''But Rosie . . .'' prompted James.

''I'm coming back to Rosie O'Grady, young man,'' she
said sharply. ''You can't expect me to get it clear all at once.
I have to sort it out a bit, don't I? I haven't talked to anybody
about Rosie since before you were born. And with all these
wicked people around me now . . .''

Her voice faded away and she began to tremble, her hands
twisting together and her head moving from side to side. Paula
almost held her breath in apprehension. If Mrs. Martyr once got
onto the subject of the proposed demolition of Railway Cottages
it would be impossible to get her off it, and it would also be
impossible not to feel a painful sympathy. The old woman had
lived too long and her little world had died around her.

There was silence in the room. The ticking of the clock
that stood at the corner of the dresser suddenly sounded very
loud. Time would not stand still and Mrs. Martyr's hours
were numbered.

''Rosie O'Grady was a very pretty girl,'' she said at last.
''She was the youngest of seven, just as I was myself, but I
was never much to look at, and I always wished I could be
like Rosie. She was tall and fair, with big blue eyes and a
cupid's bow of a mouth. And a way with her like a princess.

Somehow or other Rosie always got her own way. Her sisters did the work and Rosie played the grand lady.''

"She had admirers?'' prompted James, since Mrs. Martyr seemed once again to be deep in thought.

"Buzzed around her like flies'' was the quick reply. "But she wouldn't look at the local boys. Oh no. She was out to catch bigger fish, was our Rosie. She did learn a trade, though. Not lazy. Not when she had an object.''

'What sort of trade?'' asked James.

"A milliner. There was a salon in West Street—it's long since gone now—where they took her on. She had a good eye for fashion. She'd go and stand out in all weathers watching the nobs coming and going at the Grand Hotel and the Metropole to see what they were wearing and she'd keep it in her head and she knew what looked best with what and she was clever with her fingers. She might have done very well,'' said Mrs. Martyr sadly, "and had a little hat shop of her own one day.''

James said nothing; he knew she would go on unprompted now.

"Maybe she was hoping for better things. Or maybe she fell in love. I don't know anything about that sort of thing.''

There was another pause, and then the old woman began to laugh. "Married fifty years, brought up two sons, and buried the whole lot of them. And I've never been in love. What d'you think of that, young man?''

Paula, ignored by the other two but listening intently, thought it was terribly sad, but James was equal to it.

"It's never too late to begin,'' he said and Mrs. Martyr laughed until she had a coughing fit.

"Well, you are a beam of sunlight,'' she said when she had recovered. "I never thought to have a good laugh ever again.''

"So Rosie fell in love,'' said James thoughtfully.

"Maybe. Anyway there was a feller in it somewhere, and not one of the local lads either. Not that anybody told me at the time. Little girls weren't supposed to listen to such things. But I heard them talking, my mother and Rosie's mum and dad, and later on my mother told me the whole story. As much as she knew of it, that is. Rosie never would tell them his name, but he must have been rich enough, and probably titled too. Anyway, she had plenty of money to spend, and she took herself off to Canada—she'd always wanted to travel, she said, and she'd have the baby there. Only it wasn't just a baby. It was twins.''

"Twins!" echoed Paula, unable to restrain herself any longer.

"A boy and a girl," continued Mrs. Martyr, taking no notice of the interruption. "She wrote to her mother once to tell her they were all well, and that she'd taken up with a young Canadian feller—a Frenchie, by the sound of it—and was going to marry him and live on his farm. None of us could picture Rosie on a farm—she was always one for the big towns and the bright lights—but maybe it came to nothing. That was the last we heard of her.''

She stopped abruptly, leaned back in her chair, and shut her eyes, and her restless hands were still at last. It looked as if she had fallen asleep, and James and Paula risked looking at each other. Paula took a little memo pad from her purse, wrote on it in large letters: "The MS from this address—1949," and held it up so that James could see, praying that the old woman would not choose that moment to open her eyes.

James nodded, and they waited without speaking and without movement, looking at the tiny sleeping figure and at the blue china on the dresser and the bright-coloured rugs on the floor, and listening to the clock ticking the minutes away.

As they had hoped, Mrs. Martyr soon woke up again and seemed quite unaware that she had ever left them.

"Rosie," she murmured. "That was Rosie. I used to envy her so much. But I daresay she came to a bad end. Maybe the young Frenchman didn't marry her after all. Maybe the money ran out and she went on the streets. But she didn't write those rubbishy books you were talking about. There's no doubt of that.''

"No, I can see she didn't," agreed James. "We must have got hold of the wrong end of the stick. So you got married yourself and stayed in your old home," he went on.

"It was a perfectly good house," she said sharply. "Any man would have been glad to come and live here, especially Bert Martyr, whose mother died when he was ten and whose dad spent his time in the pub when he wasn't out in his fishing-boat.''

The tide of reminiscence flowed. Skilfully and patiently, James extracted the information that Mrs. Martyr had in fact spent one year of her life—the unhappiest year of all, she said—away from Railway Cottages. It was after the war— Hitler's war—and her husband's health had been bad and he thought he might be better in an outdoor gardening job than in the engineering workshop. So they'd gone to live on a big country estate, and let their eldest son and his wife live in the house. But when they came back, because her husband had got worse and had to give up work altogether, it was never quite the same. Her nearest acquaintances in the Cottages had gone away, and it took a long time to get used to the new people, who didn't remember the old times. And then her Bert died. . . .

The years passed, bringing more and more change and loss.

Without interrupting the flow or relaxing for one moment his attitude of sympathetic interest, James learned that the missing year was 1949; that the son and daughter-in-law who had taken over number 4 Railway Cottages for that year were both dead, and that their only child, a daughter, had never married and hardly ever came to see her grandmother, but had done very well for herself and was some sort of producer at the British Broadcasting Corporation.

Well done, James, thought Paula; another possible lead. But she was getting very sleepy in the warm little room, and beginning to wonder how they were ever going to get away.

"Your friend is tired of me," said Mrs. Martyr to James. "And so are you too, young man. You've got what you came for, haven't you? Now what am I going to get in return?"

If James was taken aback, he did not show it. "What is there that I can give you?" he asked.

She wanted him, it turned out, to help her to stay in number 4 Railway Cottages until she died, and she had a very practical proposal to make. There was a local conservation society that was fighting to preserve these old dwellings as part of the new housing estate that was to be built, and they had a good chance of winning, but they needed money to pay the lawyers. No, Mrs. Martyr could not give him their address, but she would hand over his cheque to them when they called to see her tomorrow.

Paula watched the transaction with some amusement. Unlike many well-off people, James was not miserly, but Paula could see the look of surprise on his face at the sum suggested.

When they were driving away, she said, "I'll claim it as expenses from my publishers and pay you back. In fact, you really ought to get a fee for this. I'd never have got anywhere without you."

"We'll talk about that later," said James. "The problem is—where exactly have we got?"

They had turned onto the sea front and spent some time looking for a space to park the car.

"I told you it would be even worse than London," grumbled James.

"But at least we can breathe fresh air."

"Carbon monoxide, mostly."

They got out and walked across to the short turf on the cliff-top, where there were comparatively few people. The impression of the old woman in her threatened cottage remained strongly with them.

"She lived here all her life," said Paula. "Ninety years, at least. Can you imagine?"

"Except for the year we want. Where were the later manuscripts dispatched from? Did you get that from the literary agent?"

"Everything about that first letter came from the house at Forest Brook," replied Paula. "There were two or three more letters actually signed 'Rosie O'Grady,' and then there was a letter from Robin Key, typewritten and very official, saying that Miss O'Grady wanted to concentrate on her writing and not be bothered with correspondence and that henceforth he would be handling all her affairs."

"What about the signature on the contracts?"

"That was still Rosie O'Grady."

They stood still by the wire fence at the edge of the cliff and looked out to sea. The air was warm and still, and in the hazy sunshine, sky and water blended into each other. Some little sailing boats came slowly back to the marina, and in the distance the cross-Channel ferry boat appeared from the misty horizon.

"There obviously is, or has been, a real-live Rosie O'Grady," said James, "but it doesn't look as if she wrote any novels. Did she ever come back from Canada? And if she didn't, then who was it who came to number 2 Railway Cottages during the time that Mrs. Martyr wasn't there and sent that book to a literary agency?"

"Rosie O'Grady had illegitimate twins," said Paula. "A girl and a boy. Perhaps the girl was also called Rosie, and kept the mother's name."

"Two real live Rosies?" James shook his head. "Somehow I don't buy it. I don't know why. How about this guy Robin Key?"

"Now there's a name I don't believe in," said Paula. "The key to the mystery. Somebody decided to be a bit cheeky there."

"Would he be the right age for Rosie O'Grady's boy twin?" Paula did some hasty mental calculation.

"Whoever it was who wrote the novels," she said, "was born in Canada in 1905. At least that's what was put in the biographical note, although it's not necessarily true. According to Mrs. Martyr, Rosie O'Grady—the real Rosie, I mean, not the pen-name person—had twin children in Canada at that time. If they are both alive now, they'd be over eighty. So one of them could be the woman who came to the publisher's office a few years ago, and the other could be Robin Key. George Bruce said he was getting old, and that's why he wanted me to write this book now. Rosie O'Grady the novelist is unlikely to write anything more, and Robin Key, who seems to be the only link between the novelist and the outside world, is also liable to pop off at any moment."

"If Rosie O'Grady the novelist is the girl twin, and Robin Key the general factotum is the boy twin," said James, "that would fit in very nicely, and the only mystery would be why they have been so secretive all these years."

"It's good publicity to be always trying to avoid publicity," said Paula. "It could be a deliberate build-up of secrecy to whet the appetite."

"Yes, but they weren't to know, at the beginning of their writing career, that there would be any need to publicize themselves. They didn't know they were going to be so successful when they sent in that first manuscript from number 2 Railway Cottages at the time when Mrs. Martyr—damn her—had forsaken the bright lights of Brighton to languish on a big estate in the backwoods.''

Paula made no reply, and they stood for a while in silence, staring across the now empty ocean.

''I don't like it,'' she said at last. ''This theory, I mean. Girl twin writes novels, boy twin is her manager. Why should they keep so quiet about it? They'd have got much better publicity by bringing out the whole romantic story. The whole thing is like an O'Grady novel. Poor but lovely young English girl is seduced by rich nobleman, who gives her the money to emigrate and to support the child. And it turns out to be twins. That's an original touch. Hard-working and honest young French Canadian farmer falls in love with her and marries her, twins and all. Then he dies. Then she dies. Twins, devoted to each other, decided to visit the Old Country and find the house where their mother was born. They might even want to discover who is their real father. If that was their own life story, they would have splashed it all over the first novel and everybody would have loved it.''

''You could be right.'' James yawned. ''I'm keeping an open mind until we find out some more facts. What do we do next? It's getting a bit late to go over to High Beechwoods this evening.''

''Next,'' said Paula firmly, ''we go back into Brighton and have a meal. We then go home, and tomorrow morning we try to track down Mrs. Martyr's granddaughter, who lived in number 4 Railway Cottages just after the last war and who now works at the BBC. We've started on this thing in chronological order and we might as well go on that way.''

''You're the boss,'' said James as they returned to the car. ''Personally I'd rather go and tackle Robin Key. High Beechwoods, Forest Brook. It sounds like a Gothic novel. You approach it along a rough woodland track, no other dwelling within miles. And it's surrounded by ancient beech trees and a ten-foot-high hedge. And a padlocked iron gate with a rusty bell-pull, and when you touch it there is the most terrifying sound of barking dogs, and the next minute a veritable Hound of the Baskervilles appears the other side of the gate.''

''It will probably turn out to be a semi-detached bungalow

in the middle of a very commonplace little village,'' said Paula without much conviction, for she, too, had formed a mental picture of Rosie O'Grady's residence, which was rather along the same lines as that of James.

4

That night Paula slept badly. She had discovered from her recent exercise into biography that to research into other people's lives involves a temporary surrender of some part of one's own personality. But when writing *Shadowed Lives*, she had at least had a fairly clear mental image of her subject. She knew that the people she had been writing about had really existed and she had achieved a degree of identification with them.

The case of Rosie O'Grady was very different. It was like grasping at a ghost, staring at a mirage. In the dead hours of the night Paula even began to wonder whether Mrs. Martyr had made the whole story up in order to get them to help in her campaign to preserve Railway Cottages. The old woman was very shrewd. She had realized immediately how eager for information they were, and had sold it at a high price. Even if it was not all invention, her memory could easily be at fault.

How much of what is accepted historical fact, thought Paula as she got up at half past one to make tea and smoke a cigarette, consists of just such random personal recollections? And what does it matter anyway? It is myths and fictions, not truths, that catch at people's hearts and minds and rule their lives. And that make them kill or torture other people if they don't believe the same myths, whether it is the Virgin Birth or the superiority of the Aryan Race or the Dictatorship of the Proletariat.

So if Rosie O'Grady never existed, concluded Paula, I shall

have to invent her. I've got Mrs. Martyr's story; I shall have
whatever we discover when we visit James's Gothic mansion;
and I've got the books themselves.

She stretched out a hand and picked up a paperback from
the top of the pile that she had dumped on the floor beside
her bed. On the cover was a crude and gaudy representation
of a house with turrets and gables engulfed in flames, and in
the foreground a beautiful black-haired girl in a flowing white
gown was holding a hose-pipe and appeared to be fighting
the fire single-handed. In large black capital letters at the top
was printed A ROSIE O'GRADY STORY, and underneath, in much
smaller type, *The Haunted House Mystery*.

It was the very first of the novels, the one that had been
sent to the literary agent from number 2 Railway Cottages,
Brighton, in 1949. Surely this, if nothing else, was an incon-
trovertible fact, and it seemed to Paula a good omen that it
was this story that lay on top of the pile and that she now
proposed to read right through instead of glancing at pages
at random as she had done with some of the other books.

She was a fast reader, and although she skipped nothing,
it took her barely one and a half hours. It really ought to have
been called "The Courage of Caroline" because the heroine,
a good and beautiful young girl of humble birth, performed
the most incredible heroic deeds, culminating in rescuing the
hero, the charming heir to an earldom, from the murderous
schemes of his jealous younger brother.

It was crude, absurd, naive, hackneyed—everything that a
connoisseur of literature would most despise. But it had life
in it. Having once got into the story, you wanted to read on.
Critical and contemptuous, you still read on. Whoever had
written this book possessed that vital spark, that elusive and
essential element that no amount of literary criticism would
ever be able to analyze but that outweighed every fault you
could think of.

Paula switched off the light and let her mind dwell, quite
uncritically, upon the story. Its simple certainties were like a
sweet, soothing drink. It was a rest to the tired and uneasy
mind. What would Caroline have done with a problem like
mine? was her last conscious thought.

The telephone ringing interrupted a confusion of dreams.

"Wake up, woman," said James's voice. "I've got news for you. I've found her."

"You've found Rosie?" asked Paula sleepily.

"Not yet. But we're on the way. I've found Caroline."

"Caroline?" Paula leaned over the edge of the bed and saw the gaudy cover of the book she had been reading in the small hours. "You can't have found Caroline. She's a character in one of the books."

"This one really exists," said James. "She produces radio plays. The old girl was quite right about that. I called up some people I know at the BBC last night and we're all going to meet at lunch-time today. You, me, and Caroline Martyr. Granddaughter of Mrs. Martyr of number 4 Railway Cottages, Brighton, who might just possibly remember something about the people who came to number 2 when she was living there as a young child. Are you awake now, Paula?"

"Yes," she replied, and was warm in her thanks, but at the same time she could not help feeling a trifle irritated at the way James seemed to have taken over her researches. She reminded herself that she never wanted to take on the assignment at all and that without James's help she would have discovered practically nothing, but was dismayed to find that she would not, after all, want to have his name beside her own on the title page of the biography if it ever got written.

"I am an egoist," she said to herself. "What an unpleasant discovery. But collaboration on a book is an awkward business. If two people ride one horse, one of them must ride behind."

Collaboration. Was Rosie O'Grady a team of two? A male and a female twin perhaps?

Paula spent the morning studying the paperback novels, this time bringing to bear on them the full armoury of her academic training and experience. In four out of the five novels that she looked at, she could detect no sign of any variation in the style. It was uniformly simple throughout, with short paragraphs, short sentences, plenty of dialogue but no long speeches, no ambiguities. It was as if one single clear high childlike voice was telling the tale, spinning the fantasy, the daydream.

What sort of person could be the owner of such a voice? Surely not a man. And not a sophisticated intellectual sort of female like Paula herself. Nor a tough, shrewd, and cynical old woman like Mrs. Martyr. It was the voice of innocence; the voice of self-centered, self-confident youthful innocence craving for wealth and splendour, wide open to adventure and careless of danger.

It was the voice of the pretty little milliner's apprentice who had stood in the rain near the entrance of the Grand Hotel on Brighton sea front and watched the quality coming and going in their carriages, and who had attracted the attentions of a rich young nobleman.

It was the voice of Rosie O'Grady. Old Mrs. Martyr's Rosie, the real and original Rosie, not some mythical syndicate or clever imposter.

Paula picked up the last of the five paperbacks and flicked through the pages. It was the same old story yet again. Lovely young girl from poor and humble background wins her wonder hero. The wrappings were different. This one was set in wartime. The girl was a nurse, her hero a wounded airman. The mystery concerned another nurse who caused the heroine great heartache until eventually discovered to be a spy. It all happened in a hospital "Somewhere in England," but it could have been anywhere. There was no sense of place, and the story had a timeless quality that saved it from becoming out of date.

It was the same as the other books, and yet to Paula's keen ear there seemed to be a change of tone, almost as if the author was modulating into a minor key. Perhaps it was simply that she was dealing with a sombre subject.

No, it was not only that. There was definitely a difference in the style. It was less uniform, with sentences and paragraphs varying in length, and occasionally a technical term was used that would have seemed out of place in the previous books. These words and phrases were not by any means obscure and could have been correctly used by any author who took the trouble to make a few inquiries in the right quarter. Nevertheless Paula had a strong feeling that the author of "The Courage of Caroline" would never have done any such research but would have relied on her—for surely it must be a woman—natural story-telling ability to conceal her own ignorance of the things she was writing about.

Paula made fresh coffee and lit another cigarette and sat

down to think about the last of this batch of five novels. The date of its first publication was 1955, whereas the other four had all been published before 1954, so that would fit in with the theory that there had at some point been a change of authorship. She was going to have to go through the whole lot, slowly and carefully, in chronological order, with this hypothesis in mind.

But even if she did find evidence of such a change, it would not prove that the Mystery Lady was two or more people. It might only mean a change of editor at either the literary agent's or the publisher's office. Rosie O'Grady novels had apparently always required a great deal of editing. Mistakes in grammar and punctuation and spelling had to be rectified, and the most glaring inconsistencies in the story ironed out.

Or it could even mean that the author herself had changed, become more careful, more experienced and more mature. Or perhaps when Mr. Robin Key had taken over as secretary, manager, bodyguard, or whatever else he was to Rosie, he had also taken over the polishing up of her manuscripts. In fact, the most recent books might all be his own work. Suppose Rosie was dead and Robin Key was concealing the fact, even from the publisher, and was writing the novels himself?

This sort of pretence was by no means an original theme for a literary mystery story, as Paula would have pointed out had she been reviewing such a book. But in the circumstances, she felt rather drawn to the theory. It would explain a lot, and the main objection to it was George Bruce. That he had been taken in in this manner over a long period was hardly credible, but it was equally incredible that he should have put Paula onto writing the life of the Mystery Lady if he knew that she was dead. Perhaps he suspected, but was very willing, for the sake of his firm's profits, to be deceived. After all, he had at one time sent a private inquiry agent to look into Rosie O'Grady. Why?

Paula glanced at her watch. There was just time to make two phone calls before she left for her lunch date. The first was straightforward. Frances Merivale, secretary to William Broadway, literary agent, confirmed that the procedure with all manuscripts accepted for publication, including, of course, those of Rosie O'Grady, was that the original script, edited and prepared for the printer, was returned to the author, together with the proofs for correction.

"So there aren't any original O'Grady scripts in either your office or the publisher's office?" said Paula.

"There certainly aren't any here," replied Frances, "and there would not be any with the publisher except perhaps the extra copies that go to the jacket designer. I don't know who does George Bruce's book jackets. I don't think any of them are done in the house, so presumably the script is sent to the artist. I'm sorry I can't tell you any more. Is it very important?"

"I'm working in such a fog over this book," replied Paula, "that I don't know what is important and what isn't, so I'm following up everything as it occurs to me and I thought maybe the sight of an original O'Grady manuscript might give me some inspiration."

She hoped this sounded convincing. Frances Merivale seemed to be an honest and helpful person, but Paula felt that it was wise not to drop any hint about her theory that there had been some sort of conspiracy to suppress the fact of Rosie's death. Or to suppress the fact that the Mystery Lady was some sort of composite character or even a sequence of characters.

George Bruce wanted a biography full of human interest, and Mrs. Martyr's revelations suggested the lines along which such a life could be written. Even if Paula did discover that Rosie's career had been a fraud, it would not necessarily matter, for in art and in literature it is so often the forger who is the hero to the general public. But there must on no account be the slightest suspicion that George himself had any part in the fraud. That would never be forgiven, either by Rosie's millions of readers or by George Bruce himself.

Paula picked up the telephone again. The operator put her straight through to George. At least he is accessible, she thought, and doesn't play the hard-to-get-tycoon. But she had not prepared herself for the conversation and she put her questions clumsily and nervously. The answers she received were disturbing, perhaps even a little alarming, and Paula decided to tell James about this conversation as soon as possible. It was good, after all, to have his co-operation and support.

During the bus ride to the West End, Paula's mind was full
of George Bruce and his bullying and devious methods, and
it was an effort to switch to the coming meeting. She felt very
little in the mood for talking to Mrs. Martyr's granddaughter,
who would no doubt turn out to be very elegant and sophisticated, whereas Paula had been so busy reading and thinking
all morning that she barely had time to make herself presentable.

They met, to her relief, not in a crowded bar full of media
people but in the comparative peace and comfort of the restaurant of a Bond Street Department Store, and Mrs. Martyr's
granddaughter was not at all as Paula had expected. She was
short and plump and had a nervous habit of smoothing down
her black springy hair as she talked.

"Granny has never forgiven me for not producing a litter
of great-grandchildren," she said when Paula mentioned their
visit to Mrs. Martyr. "She doesn't approve of my life-style
at all and my trips to Brighton are not very agreeable to either
of us. But I make sure she gets visited by a social worker and
I'm in touch with the Preservation Society. It would kill her
to be rehoused."

"You lived for a while in Railway Cottages yourself, didn't
you?" said Paula. "I was hoping you might remember something from that time."

"Yes. James told me." Caroline glanced at the menu,
asked for salad and coffee, and continued. "I'm afraid I'm
not going to be much help. I was only five or six years old
and I can't remember it clearly, except that it felt terribly
small and shut-in after the village in Devon where my mother
and I had been living while my father was on active service
in the Middle East. My parents were unhappy there too. It
was a bad time. But it's not my life you're researching," she
added briskly. "James said you're trying to find out who was
living at number 2 at that time. The O'Grady house."

A middle-aged waitress brought their orders.

"The O'Grady house," repeated Caroline thoughtfully after she had gone. "It is difficult to sort out the myth from the
reality. I suppose my grandparents and my parents must have
talked about the family. The handsome and headstrong
O'Gradys. They weren't Irish, you know. At least not for
several generations. They'd been in Brighton for a long time,

but by the end of the war they'd nearly all died or gone away. One of them actually died when we were there. An old man. It was not to be spoken of in front of the children—that was me—but I got it from the other kids in the neighbourhood. He was found dead and I think there was something suspicious about it."

"A corpse," exclaimed James. "It's high time we came across a corpse in this investigation."

"I'm afraid there's nothing particularly exciting about it," said Caroline. "As far as I can remember, the old man died in a room full of gas. It used to be coal gas in those days, which really was lethal. My granny refused to use any. She did everything on the old kitchen range until about five years ago, when I managed to smuggle in an electric kettle and a tiny electric cooker. She'd die rather than admit she ever uses them, but I'm quite sure she does."

"My grandmother was like that too," said Paula.

"And mine," said James, "lived in great luxury with every possible labour-saving device plus a non-resident housekeeper. Isn't it odd that we three people, a random selection, should all have been dominated by our grandmothers?"

They all pondered this for a moment, and then James brought them back to the Railway Cottages corpse.

"There's not much to tell," said Caroline. "I don't even know who it was, but I think it must have been one of the O'Grady brothers. The only one left there." She paused to drink some coffee, then said, "If I knew what you two were investigating, it might help a bit. I don't know whether you want me to meander along with vague memories, or whether you'd like to hear my own theories about the O'Grady family."

Paula and James looked at each other. "I thought you'd explained to Caroline," said Paula.

"You said it was meant to be hush-hush," said James virtuously, "and you're the boss in this enterprise."

"Shall I guess and save you embarrassment?" suggested Caroline. "It can't be a sequel to *Shadowed Lives*, can it, Paula? But it must be something literary. The O'Grady household. That strikes a bell."

"Rosie," said James. "The romantic novelist."

"You think she's one of the Railway Cottages clan? Wow,"

said Caroline, and there came into her eyes the speculative
look of one who scents a good story. "It never occurred to
me to make the connection," she added, "but it isn't my
type of reading, and I've never worked on any of the book
programmes. But if you came up with the solution to the
Mystery Lady—"

"Don't let's get too excited," said Paula. "It's probably
something so dreary and uninteresting that even George Bruce
won't want to publish it."

"But at least we've got a corpse," said Caroline, "as James
says; and now that I know what it's all about, I can tell you
how I think it happened."

5

James ordered more coffee. The restaurant was emptying, shoppers and office workers alike returning to their labours. The waitresses retired to their own quarters and Paula and her companions sat like conspirators under the potted palms in the corner by the millinery department, where customers were few and far between.

"Well, here's my theory about the last of the O'Gradys," said Caroline, "derived from what I remember myself and what the neighbourhood children were saying and what I heard my parents say, but it's probably unreliable because I was always accused of having my head in a book and being unconscious of my surroundings. Which is true. I was a snob and a social climber from the age of four, and I hated my working-class background and wanted to get out of it. Which I did," she added defiantly.

"I was inclined to be the same," said Paula, and they smiled at each other rather nervously before Caroline went on.

"I think two of the O'Gradys died in the First World War, and another two of them emigrated to Australia. Then there was Rosie, that's five, and another girl who made a prosperous marriage and got away—I don't know where—and just this old man left who was the eldest, I think. He was a bit of a scandal. Drank heavily and never married but had a series of lady friends living there. I bet my granny didn't tell you that."

"No, she said nothing about it," agreed James.

"She knew about it, though, and she knew about the old man's death, but perhaps she decided that it wasn't relevant

36

or that you'd had enough for your money. Well, the current lady friend—she was a boozy old dame, I guess—found him dead in this room full of gas and raised hell in the middle of the night, banging on all the neighbours' doors, including ours, and it was actually my father who got up and went for the police. It was recorded as an accidental death. He'd come in drunk and turned on the gas fire and forgotten to put a match to it. The woman ought to have been with him, but apparently they'd had a quarrel and she'd taken herself off elsewhere and then relented and returned at three in the morning. Naturally everybody suspected that she'd done it, and all sorts of rumours were going around. People said he had a small fortune in one-pound notes hidden about the house, and she wasn't going to move out until she'd found every one of them. My parents thought there could be some truth in this. People of that type did keep a surprising amount of cash under the mattress or shoved into old teapots or down inside the grandfather clock.''

Caroline paused for a moment.

"Money,'' said James thoughtfully. "What about papers, documents, manuscripts?''

"Presumably those too, if they seemed to be of any value,'' said Caroline. "But don't forget this is all conjecture. I'm quite sure Granny could tell you more if she would, even though she wasn't living there at the time.''

"So this woman,'' said James, "could have come across the manuscript of that first O'Grady novel and sent it off to a literary agent as if it were her own work?''

"Yes, if these conjectures are true,'' replied Caroline, "though it seems wildly unlikely. She doesn't sound to be anything like the sort of person who would know enough to realize that there could be money in a manuscript, let alone know what to do with it.''

The others agreed with her.

"Whoever wrote to William Broadway,'' said Paula, "certainly knew something about publishing. Could the boozy old dame have had some literary friends? It doesn't sound very likely either.''

"Wait a minute,'' said Caroline. "You haven't heard the end of the story. She was turned out of the cottage eventually by a much younger woman who claimed to be the niece of the old man who died and who stayed on there for some time, clearing up the mess and presumably searching for any cash that had escaped the eye of the other.''

"The niece," said Paula, and James added, ''Whose child?''

They waited for an answer, but Caroline did not know and could not guess. Nor had she much more to tell. The last of the O'Gradys, as Paula was mentally titling the presumed niece, did not stay in Railway Cottages for many weeks, but put the house into the care of an estate agent, who took a long time to find a purchaser, and by the time it was inhabited again, Caroline's parents had gone back to London, her grandmother had returned to her own home, and the residents of Railway Cottages had other things to talk about than the goings on at number 2. The years passed, bringing many more changes, until it was only Caroline's grandmother who remembered the O'Grady clan at all.

When she had finished speaking, the three of them remained quiet for a little while in the now empty restaurant. Then Caroline said that she had to get back to work, and they parted with many expressions of thanks and promises to keep in touch.

"We're not much further forward, though," said James as he and Paula walked along one of the quieter side streets of Mayfair in the direction of Hyde Park. "The niece could have sent the original manuscript. Or the boozy old man or one of his lady friends. Or even, come to that, one of the estate agents' clerks.''

"But the niece cleared out the house," objected Paula.

"There could have been some rubbishy old pieces of furniture that even she didn't want, and a lot of old papers tucked away in them.''

"I suppose so," said Paula doubtfully, "although if someone suspects that money is hidden somewhere . . . But in any case, they all sound equally unlikely people to have sent the book to the agent, and even more unlikely that any of them actually wrote it. And unless Caroline turns up with something a bit more specific, I don't see how we can follow up any of those trails at all.''

They walked a little way in silence, and then Paula continued: "There's something I want to tell you, James. Are you in a hurry to go anywhere?"

"I ought to be going home. I'm supposed to be writing a longish review of that new book on George Eliot and it's already overdue, but I suppose they'll forgive me."

"They'll forgive you, James. Everyone always does. Let's go and sit by the Serpentine and look at ducks."

" 'From troubles of the world I turn to ducks,' " he said, grabbing Paula's hand and pulling her after him through the narrow gaps between the throbbing, stationary buses in Park Lane.

On the bank of the lake under the willow trees the air felt comparatively clean and the traffic noise was a not unpleasant distant hum. James found a park bench, saying he was too old to sit on the grass.

"I thought you were a trifle distrait during lunch," he remarked, "but I don't think Caroline noticed. After all, she doesn't know you as I do."

These last words seemed to Paula to contain a threat of some sentimental reminiscing that could strain their comfortable friendship. She hastened to tell him about her morning's researches.

"I ought to have read all the novels immediately when I took on the job," she said. "I'm being very disorganized about the whole thing."

"You can't make plans in a case like this," said James soothingly. "You just have to follow your instincts. What happened when you called George Bruce?"

"Oh, I made a mess of that too. I just asked him why he had never told me he once put a private detective onto Rosie. Just blurted it out."

"Did you tell him where you'd heard that?"

"I don't think so, but he'd know it must have been somebody in his office or in the literary agent's. Actually it was William Broadway's secretary."

"And what was the elderly whiz-kid publisher's reply to your questions?"

"Very breezy and offhand. Oh, that old story. That was years ago. It was to quell a rumour that some spiteful rival publisher had started that the famous Mystery Lady was not an author, but a syndicate."

"Sounds very possible," commented James, "but why didn't George Bruce tell you this when he dumped the job on you?"

"The answer was that he wanted me to come to it with a completely open mind, not lumbered with somebody else's theories."

"That's absurd. No one would ever do any research on anything at all if it weren't for somebody else's theories."

"Exactly. I told him so, and he made his usual sarcastic remarks about the academic mind; but I managed to stick to it, although I'm really rather scared of him, you know, James, and he said that he had satisfied himself that there really was a reclusive old lady living at Rosie's address. So he managed to scotch the rumours, and Rosie—if it really was Rosie— actually visited his office and William Broadway's office some years ago. Didn't I tell you?"

"You described it most vividly. Sounds to me like a *Charley's Aunt* type of impersonation. However, did you ask George what detective agency he used?"

"Good Lord, no. And he'll make damn sure I don't find out. I'm not going to start my own investigations into George Bruce. Not on top of the O'Grady mystery itself. That way madness lies."

"I don't know," said James thoughtfully. "It sounds a very profitable line of inquiry. But if you're going to come up against George Bruce's own obstruction . . . what an extraordinary business, to set you on the trail and then block off one of the main avenues. Can you make sense of it?"

"I've got to assume," replied Paula, leaning forward and staring broodingly at the upended rear of a young mallard a couple of feet from the bank, "that George Bruce genuinely does not know anything about the author of the O'Grady books and genuinely hopes that I can produce some sort of sensational biography. Or else expose a conspiracy. I have to assume that. Otherwise I'll have to give up the job."

"Oh, don't do that," cried James with feeling. "Please don't give up the job. It would mean we wouldn't meet so often, and I'm so much enjoying it. It's like getting to know you all over again."

There was a silence. James seemed to realize that he had strayed beyond the agreed limits of their friendship. He picked up a small stone and tossed it lightly into the water. The young duck turned somersault and splashed indignantly away.

"We ought to have brought some cake crumbs," said Paula.

"They're disgustingly overfed," said James.

The danger moment had passed, but Paula feared that it could come again and that she might even be tempted herself. After all, she had at one time been very much in love with him. James must hurry up and find another woman, she decided, to replace the Chinese girl who had defected. She said this aloud. That was one of the nicest things about James, that you could say anything you liked to him and he never took offence or got hurt. He did not, however, simply laugh it off as she had expected, but returned to a more subtle attack.

"And how about you finding another man, so that we can continue our brother-and-sister act?"

"I don't want to," said Paula.

"Why?"

Paula made no reply.

"Because of Richard? I thought it was you who gave him the push. Wasn't it?"

"Yes," said Paula miserably.

"You did the right thing there," went on James. "Okay, so he's a fine scholar and underneath all that prickliness he's a decent-enough human being, but he'd want to make you over into his ideal of you. Tidy you up and stop you smoking so much, to begin with. And after that he'd go to work on your mind. You'd never have descended to the novels of Rosie O'Grady if you stuck with Richard, would you?"

"Oh, do shut up, James!" cried Paula. "I don't want to be analysed. I've got a job to do."

"So you're delving into other people's lives in order to avoid having to cope with your own. All right, I'll go along with it, but I warn you—we're coming back to the subject of Paula Glenning one of these days, because I'm fond of mysteries too, and you're a mystery to me and I guess to yourself as well."

Paula remained silent. She was leaning forward again, resting her face on her hands and staring at a fresh supply of ducks. For most of the time nowadays she enjoyed a full and

active life, with work she liked and many friends and interests, and with her sister's home and family as a light little
anchor. She told herself that she was not capable of any lasting love or permanent relationship, and that she had come to
terms with the fact. There were to be no more highs and lows
in her life. Looking forward from the age of forty, she was
going to spread her emotions thinly over a wide area instead
of concentrating them all on one place or one person. That
was sensible, wasn't it, when you knew that you were con-
stitutionally incapable of adjusting yourself to anybody else?

Yet every now and then she would be attacked by this overwhelming sense of pointlessness and of despair, as if there
were no light or colour in the world. It came to her now,
sitting by the lake in Hyde Park on a bright summer afternoon, looking across at the golden-green cascade of willow
branches and the brown-speckled backs of the ducks on the
muddy water.

Nothingness. No sense or meaning anywhere. It came
without warning and her reason told her that it would pass,
but while it lasted it was bad. This time it seemed to be
particularly bad, and the presence of such a good friend made
it even worse. It was not James's fault; it could have come
just the same if he had not been there, but since he was there,
and since she now suspected, in the midst of her own darkness, that he went through such black times too, she must
resist this impulse to grab hold of him and say, "Help me,
James, I'm lonely as well," because it would only start the
cycle all over again and destroy their precious foothold of
goodwill and trust that they had reached together.

The impulse passed, and the blackness began to lift, but
Paula felt weakened and rather ashamed, as if she had made
a cowardly contract to keep away from life for fear of being
hurt. In twenty or thirty years' time, maybe, it would make
sense, but she was not old enough for such a contract, and
maybe James, still willing to risk entanglement, was the
braver of the two of them.

They returned to Rosie O'Grady on the bus going back to
Hampstead.

"I shall have to call her direct," said Paula. "I can't put
it off any longer. The fact is, I'm being cowardly, James. I'm
scared of High Beechwoods. I've a horrible suspicion that

your Hound of the Baskervilles idea is right and that George
Bruce won't tell me what happened to his detective because
it would put me off.''

"We'll go there tomorrow and get it over with," said
James.

As soon as she was back in her own haven, Paula took out
of the still very slim O'Grady file the letter to Robin Key that
the publisher had given her.

"This is to introduce Dr. Paula Glenning, of the University of London, who is undertaking a study of the writings of
Miss O'Grady. She is a Lecturer in English Literature and an
accomplished literary critic, but while her primary interest is
in the novels themselves, it would be helpful to her to have a
little information about the author. . . .''

No suggestion was made that Paula might actually want to
meet Rosie herself. All the emphasis was on the novels, not on
the life. But would Robin Key be taken in? Surely not. He had
dealt with George Bruce for many years and would know just
what he wanted. And if Robin Key was a reader himself, he
would probably have heard something about Paula's book *Shadowed Lives*, and would know perfectly well that it was the same
sort of probing biography that she was working on now.

No. The introduction letter was designed less to smooth
Paula's way than to cover George if anything went wrong.

A woman's voice answered when Paula called the High
Beechwoods number. It spoke with a strong foreign accent.
"Mr. Key not here."

"When will he be in?"

"Not here," repeated the voice.

"Then can I speak to the secretary?"

"Not here. I clean house," said the voice.

Paula tried again. "Is Miss O'Grady available?"

"I take message. Call you back. Who speaking?"

"George Bruce's office. Miss O'Grady's publisher," said
Paula in desperation. "It's rather urgent."

There was a silence. Then the voice began again.

"Mr. Key not here."

Paula swore, slammed down the telephone, and spent the
rest of the day making detailed notes on the difference in style
in the O'Grady novels.

6

"We turn off the main road here," said Paula.

James disagreed. He prided himself on his map-reading and sense of direction. They drove on for several miles before he admitted, in a roundabout way, that she had been right. A series of sharp corners and very narrow lanes brought them back to the place that Paula had indicated. She made no comment. She was so grateful for his company that she could afford to be indulgent.

Forest Brook appeared suddenly, at the bottom of a steep hill. It consisted of a few nondescript cottages; an unattractive inn, very much shut; a stream in which had collected an old tyre and some rusty tins; and a petrol pump beside which sat the only sign of life in the place. This was an old man smoking a pipe and reading the back page of the *Daily Mirror*.

"Lost your way?" he said as James got out of the car. "Over the bridge, straight up the hill, turn right at the top, and that will bring you out onto the A-22."

And he replaced the pipe in his mouth and returned to the sports page. James looked at Paula helplessly and she got out to join him.

"This is Forest Brook, isn't it?" she asked.

"Yes," said the old man without looking up.

"Then we're in the right place. We're looking for a house called High Beechwoods. Do you know it?"

"Over the bridge, up the hill past the farm, then turn left

along the cart-track at the top,'' he replied with a complete lack of interest.

"Thanks," said James brusquely, and added to Paula as they drove up the hill, "Ought we to have tried to get something out of him?"

"I doubt if we'd have succeeded. But it's very odd," she said. "If you were a celebrity seeking privacy, you'd choose a house in or near a pleasant but not touristy village. As Kipling did. And Virginia Woolf. You wouldn't come to a dump like Forest Brook."

"Maybe the house itself is something special," said James without conviction.

"Turn left here," said Paula, and this time he instantly obeyed her.

It was a long and stony track and James grieved aloud for his tyres. At the end was a small red-roofed bungalow surrounded by a high privet hedge and backed by a slope of beech trees, now in their bright summer green. Outside the wooden gate, and blocking their way, stood a red mini, not new but clean and in good condition.

"So where is our Gothic mansion?" said James.

"In our minds, together with the guard dogs," said Paula, getting out of the car. "But there's a nice black cat."

She bent down to stroke it, but after a quick sniff at her ankles, the cat trotted off down the track.

"Belongs at the farm," said a man's voice close by. "We don't encourage it here."

It was a firm, clear voice, and both James and Paula, in the second that they were turning round, formed a mental image of iron-gray hair, ancient tweeds, and aristocratic features.

They were wrong on all counts. The owner of the well-bred voice was not very tall. He was almost bald, was wearing a dark-grey suit, and had a small, monkey-like face.

"What can I do for you?" he said, not with hostility but without any appearance of friendliness.

Paula took an envelope out of her shoulder-bag. "I have a letter of introduction from George Bruce to Mr. Key," she said.

"You may hand it to me," said the man. He glanced at the letter and then turned back to Paula. "You come at a somewhat inauspicious time. Miss O'Grady has been taken ill and is in a nursing home. I have a little business to attend to here, and shall then be going to see her. However, rather than that you should have a wasted journey—''

He broke off, held open the gate for them, and jerked his head in a peremptory manner towards the front door of the bungalow. They walked past a lawn bordered with red geraniums. It was well-kept, but had the impersonal air of a city park. Inside the bungalow Paula had the sense of a show-house, furnished by a real estate company for the benefit of prospective purchasers in the middle-income ranges. They sat in a room overlooking the lawn and the beechwoods beyond. There was a light-grey carpet, crimson chairs and curtains, a small writing desk on which stood a portable typewriter, covered, and two long, low bookcases. Paula took a roundabout way to one of the chairs in order to glance at the shelves. They appeared to contain nothing but O'Grady novels in a variety of English-language editions and in translation. On the pale-grey walls hung reproductions of Constable landscapes, and on a glass-topped coffee table stood a heavy glass ashtray and a bowl of wilting roses.

These drooping flowers were, to Paula, the only sign of human habitation in the room. Otherwise the place was like a stage set. Even the view from the window had a claustrophobic effect, as if the lawn and the beech trees were painted on a backdrop.

Paula introduced James. The short, bald, elderly man, who now announced himself as Robin Key, turned from one to the other as he replied.

"You must excuse my not offering any refreshment. The housekeeper has been given leave of absence, since Miss O'Grady seems likely to be away for some time, but I can spare you a few minutes. What exactly do you need to know, Mrs. Glenning?''

"The thing that interests me above all," replied Paula, "is who has been writing the O'Grady books ever since the first four novels.''

The question was beating at her mind, but she had certainly not meant to say it aloud. She had intended to be cautious and polite, keeping up the pretense, reining in her own impulsiveness, following along any path that Robin Key chose to point out to her. She heard James speak her name in a low warning voice; she heard the other man say, very coolly, "Ah yes, the change of style," and she heard herself continue, clearly and precisely, as if she were giving a lecture.

"I admit that I have not yet made a complete study of every one of the novels, but I have read enough to have gained a strong impression that the Rosie O'Grady novels have not all been written by the same person. The first published novel— originally entitled 'The Courage of Caroline'—establishes the authentic O'Grady voice. Naive, enthusiastic, unmistakably sincere. The Cinderella story, told with great immediacy and with a certain gift of observation by somebody who believed in the myth, possibly even lived it in her own life. The following three books are variations on the same theme, but the voice remains true. Then comes the change. It would not be noticed—in fact, it obviously was not noticed—by anybody who had formed firm expectations of what a Rosie O'Grady story ought to be. The readers would not notice. Whether the editors—people dealing professionally with words—noticed or not is a question I can't even attempt to answer, but I am quite sure that the change of style is due to a very fundamental change of author's voice, and not simply to a change of editor in her publishing house."

She paused for breath.

James said, "But, Paula—" and stopped again, shifting anxiously in his chair.

Robin Key said nothing. He sat opposite Paula, his hands clasped lightly, his face expressionless, looking at her and listening.

"A good reviewer would have noticed," Paula went on, "but books like these seldom get reviewed, so that didn't arise. And a teacher of English Literature like myself was bound to notice, but I don't suppose the books have ever been subjected to this sort of analysis before. Academic studies of popular writers tend not to be made until after the author's death."

Paula stopped speaking as abruptly as she had begun. She had very nearly added, "But of course Rosie O'Grady is dead," and she had only just enough presence of mind to stop herself.

"One could quote examples to the contrary," said Robin

Key, "but I agree that, in general, academic people tend not to interest themselves in lowbrow best-selling authors at the height of their fame. Could it be that they are afraid of becoming contaminated by such trash if they examine it too closely?"

James, less agitated at this moment than Paula, looked closely at the old man. The voice had contained no suggestion of sarcasm, and the small, squashed features gave no clue as to what he was thinking. Only one thing was sure: Here was a formidable intelligence, and James, who was good at making quick superficial contacts with people but less good at breaking down a hostile reserve, knew that he could be of no help. Paula must do the best she could. Perhaps, after all, she had some sort of plan of campaign and was not just stumbling recklessly along.

At least she had succeeded in getting Robin Key talking instead of uttering a few formal sentences and then dismissing them.

"I don't think I've worried about being contaminated," Paula was saying. "It's just that there's so much good writing to study that it seems a pity to waste time on the other sort."

"But on this occasion you have been persuaded to do so. Why is that?"

"I don't really know," replied Paula. "Money, I suppose."

"And George Bruce is very persuasive." Robin Key sounded mildly amused. "I will give you an example of his talents which will at the same time answer your query about the change of style and then I am afraid I really must go. I have a long drive ahead and I tire easily nowadays."

James looked at Paula, mentally urging her to ask Robin Key where he was going, for surely this was the moment for a direct question that could well produce a lie that might give them a clue. But Paula was leaning forward with an expression of eager interest on her face, ready to take in anything she was told. She is fascinated by his subtleties, thought James in disgust. Paula's no actress: She really wants to hear, and he began to wish that he had, after all, taken over the questioning himself.

Robin Key spoke with every appearance of frankness. "George Bruce was not satisfied with Miss O'Grady's fifth manuscript, and he told me so. It was at this time that I took over the management of her affairs, although I did not actually move into this house until sometime later. But that is beside the point. It is not my own life and work that we are discussing.''

''Oh, but we are!'' cried James, unable to restrain himself any longer.

Paula glanced at him reproachfully, and Robin Key continued as if there had been no interruption.

''The early O'Grady books had required a lot of editing in order to be made publishable. One of William Broadway's assistants—a very clever lady—looked after this, and by the time the scripts came to George Bruce they were ready for the printer. But the assistant retired from the job—she was quite elderly—and the next manuscript was sent to George Bruce exactly as it stood. He contacted me and asked what was to be done. The work was hopeless as it was, but the readers had been promised another O'Grady novel and he couldn't think of a suitable person to do the salvaging of the manuscript. The upshot was a long conference between myself and George Bruce in his office. A tough bargaining session. There is no record of this conversation and I cannot now remember the details, but the gist of the agreement, which remains to this day a purely verbal one, was that I should undertake to convey the novels to him, via the literary agent, in publishable form, and that in return he should do two things.

''The first was, more favourable financial arrangements. The second was that Miss O'Grady, who has always had an aversion to personal publicity that amounts almost to phobia, should never be harassed nor bullied nor in any way persuaded into any such publicity whatever. Up till now, both of us have kept faithfully to this unwritten agreement, and I am at this moment trying to make up my mind whether the fact that George Bruce has commissioned you to undertake a study of the O'Grady novels does or does not constitute a breach of the agreement. I had no idea that he was contemplating such a move.''

He looked keenly at Paula, who said nothing. James, knowing her well, thought that it was written all over her that her job was to write not about the novels, but almost the Mystery Lady herself.

"Thank you for being so frank with me," said Paula at last. "That certainly does explain the change of style. Of course I can't help wondering who you got to do the rewriting."

"Of course you can't," agreed Robin Key blandly. "It makes rather a nonsense of literary criticism, doesn't it, when the object of study turns out to be the result of massive and skilful editing instead of the much-venerated author's own authentic inspiration."

The mockery in his voice was now very evident. James admired Paula for ignoring it.

"It also makes nonsense of George Bruce's letter of introduction," she said in her most straightforward manner. "The only person who will ever be qualified to write a study of the O'Grady novels is you yourself."

"Very true. And I have no intention of doing so. I cannot imagine that anybody would be the least bit interested in reading it. The transformation of disorderly literary trash into orderly literary trash is hardly an enthralling topic. Of course, if it were a question of Miss O'Grady's actual life, that would be a very different matter. In such cases the public appetite is voracious. That would be much more in the George Bruce tradition, but I hardly think he would risk breaking our agreement to such a degree. He would be too afraid that I might retaliate."

There was a silence. The word "retaliate," with its hint of threat, seemed to linger on in the quiet room. It was as if the three of them, locked in this timeless and placeless stage set, were unsure what to do next, awaiting their cue.

At last Robin Key got to his feet. Paula followed suit. "I am sorry to have taken up so much of your time, Mr. Key," she said. "There seems to be some sort of misunderstanding here, and I think I had better clear it up with George Bruce before I go any further with my studies."

"That would probably be your best plan," said Robin Key gravely.

They moved towards the front door.

"I hope Miss O'Grady will soon be better," said Paula formally.

"Thank you. One must hope so. But severe heart attacks at her age and in her condition do not offer a very good prognosis."

"So the O'Grady books will soon come to an end in any case. Unless one of your clever editors—"

"I think you may safely assume, Mrs. Glenning, that there will not be any new books by Rosie O'Grady. Nor will there ever be any published Life. George Bruce knows that as well as I do, and perhaps you will kindly convey the message to him when you see him. Are you intending to return to London now? If so, your best way is—"

James interrupted him. "As it's such a fine day, I think we'll explore a little. Is there some place near here where we can get a meal?"

Robin Key made suggestions and gave directions.

"And don't forget my message to George Bruce" were his parting words.

7

Almost opposite the track that led to High Beechwoods was another path, even more grassy and bumpy, that lost itself after a few yards in a thick hazel copse. James backed the White Rover, with some difficulty, into this unpromising by-way, wincing as the branches scratched the side of the car, but nevertheless continuing in reverse.

"He said the pub was through the village," said Paula.

"I know, but I think we ought to follow him. With any luck he won't see us here when he comes out."

"But you can't follow him," objected Paula. "He'll know at once."

"I'll keep a long way behind. This car's got twice the speed of the mini."

"And it's twice as conspicuous. Oh dear." Paula leaned back in the passenger seat and began to laugh weakly. "This is absurd. Besides, I really do need a drink."

"Here he comes," muttered James, craning forward. "He's gone towards the Hastings road."

Paula resigned herself to the chase. After all, it couldn't last very long. In these narrow winding lanes, it was the tiny car that had the advantage. The Rover would be useless if they were to encounter something coming the other way. Only by complicated manoeuvres would they be able to sort themselves out, and by that time surely even James would realize that there was no point in going on.

But James was lucky, as he so often was. They saw no other vehicle until they had reached a wider road.

"London or the coast?" said James.

"London," said Paula firmly.

James immediately turned the other way and a few minutes later exclaimed in triumph.

Paula caught a glimpse of a red mini a long way ahead. There were a number of vehicles in between.

"How do you know it's his?" she asked rather irritably.

"I got the number."

"But you can't possibly read it at this distance."

James took no notice. He was obviously enjoying himself. "There's some chocolate somewhere if you need sustenance," he said cheerfully. "Ah. The motorway. Do you know," he added a moment later, "I've got a feeling he's going to Dover."

Paula roused herself to study road signs and distances. The stream of traffic that they were in did indeed seem to her to have a purposeful air, as of drivers heading for their holidays. For a little while her thoughts wandered. James was good company. Why didn't they take the touring holiday through France down to Spain that they had sometimes talked about, but never achieved, during the time they had been together? It would be much pleasanter now. No deep emotional involvement, and no making do with third-rate hotels, because they both liked to be comfortable. Paula realized with a shock that she, at least, had changed in this respect. Not so many years ago, creature comforts would have mattered little to her. Was it a sign of getting older that they mattered now? Or was it because of something rather more disturbing, that the less one felt able to commit oneself to any close relationship with anybody, the more one craved physical luxury?

I must ask James about this, she said to herself; he's had a very easy and comfortable life; he ought to know.

"He's still there," cried James joyfully. "I thought so."

Paula had been aware of their burst of speed but still not fully conscious of her surroundings. With an effort she pulled herself out of her own reflections.

"Dover, fifty," she read from the big blue notice ahead of them. "I guess you're right, James. That is, always supposing we are following the right car."

"It's the right car," he said confidently.

Ten miles later Paula said, "And what are we going to do when we get to Dover?"

"I don't know." For the first time James sounded rather at a loss. "Have you got your passport with you?"

"No. Why should I? Have you?"

James made no reply, and for the next ten miles neither of them spoke.

Then Paula said, "If by any chance it does turn out that we have been following Robin Key, and if we do manage to discover which of the cross-Channel ferries he has driven onto, what are we going to do about it? We'll be there soon and we ought to have some kind of plan."

"I believe you can do day-trips to Calais without a passport," said James vaguely.

"I believe you can, but I'm not sure about the car. Do you really suppose that Robin Key is going to make a day-trip to Calais?"

"No, I suppose not," said James so disconsolately that Paula felt obliged to comfort him.

"At least we'll have found out that he's gone abroad. And since he's bound to have realized by now that we've been chasing him, we might as well try to speak to him and ask where he's going. We ought to be watching out to see whether he goes to the East Docks or the West Docks."

"Yes." James cheered up immediately at the prospect of something definite to do. "I'll get a bit nearer."

They overtook a number of slower-moving vehicles, leaving only a small French car and a battered-looking Dormobile between themselves and the red mini.

"If he didn't know before, he certainly knows now," said Paula, laughing. "But I think you're right, James. I think I got the number."

She repeated it and he nodded. "I was afraid he'd turn off somewhere, and try to lose us."

"Why should he? He knows we can't follow him onto the ferry."

"But we can if we buy day-returns."

"Oh no, James. Please."

They argued the rest of the way. James was convinced that they could talk to Robin Key on the boat and get something more out of him. At the very least, they would know in which direction he would be driving when they got to Calais or Ostend.

Paula retorted that Robin Key would obviously go straight to a cabin and shut himself away, and would send for the purser or some such authority if they tried to pester him; that it would be of very little use to know which motorway he was taking when they got to the other side, and that the last thing they wanted was to get tangled up with the French or Belgian customs and passport control if they missed the boat they were supposed to be coming back on.

James had to admit that it would probably end up in some such nuisance.

"Bloody passports," he muttered. "What's the use of the European Economic Community then?"

Paula felt half-relieved and half-disappointed at having gained her point. Part of her was enjoying the chase. It made her feel young and irresponsible.

"West Docks," she said. "He's going right round the round-about."

"Ferry or hovercraft?"

The traffic was slowing down now, getting in line for the ocean terminals. For a little while they lost the mini completely and Paula found herself becoming as agitated as James.

"Sealink ferry," she said at last. "That ought to be easier to get at him."

But James was not listening. He had wound down the window and was talking to a man in a shabby navy-blue uniform.

"Tickets?" inquired Paula anxiously.

"Yes, but we can go into the parking lot. It's the Ostend ferry and they'll let them on in ten minutes. There he is."

Nobody seemed to be organizing the waiting vehicles. The White Rover shot in front of a slow-moving van and came to a halt only inches away from Robin Key's car.

Paula, suddenly feeling all over again the absurdity of their own behaviour, was glad to hide behind James and let him speak. He was leaning out of the window, tapping on the glass of the mini. Paula stared ahead with great concentration at an unattractive-looking hut that housed a snack-bar. Robin Key had opened his window and James was saying something. The noise of throbbing engines was so loud that she could not hear what it was. Cars were moving on towards the ferry boat. The driver behind the Rover was hooting, but James did not move on. Paula shut her eyes. She had always had a horror of public scenes and recriminations with strangers. The hooting became louder, and was joined by shouting before James shifted at last, and even then they spent some minutes blocking the line of incoming vehicles and arousing a great deal more hostility before they could get out of the docks.

In the comparative peace of a short shopping street they found a place to relax.

"Well?" said Paula.

"It wasn't wasted effort," replied James. "I'll tell you when we've found somewhere to have a drink."

"The pubs will be closed."

"Damn. Coffee bar?"

Paula nodded, and they came from bright sunshine into semi-darkness. The only other people in the little café were a couple of disconsolate-looking purple-haired punks, an old woman who appeared to be asleep, and a yawning girl at the self-service counter.

James brought a tray to the table where Paula was sitting. "The tea looked slightly less revolting," he said, "and I thought the cheese sandwiches would probably be the safest."

Paula began to laugh. James looked up in surprise.

"I'd just been thinking," she explained, "that you and I were both rather fond of our creature comforts."

"I am," said James, "but I didn't think you were."

"Which makes it all the greater sacrifice on your part. I've never thanked you properly for taking all this time and trouble over my researches."

"I've always wanted to be in a car chase," he said. "And it was worth it. Truly. I asked him straight out where he was going. There wasn't time for any subtleties."

"Did he tell you to mind your own business?"

"No. He seemed rather agitated." James hesitated.

"Hardly surprising after that drive," commented Paula. "He's not a young man."

"No. I thought he looked rather wan. He said it was his job to protect Miss O'Grady from unwelcome intrusions into her privacy, and would I please pass that message on to you and to George Bruce. I said I thought he was on his way to see her in a nursing home, and he said that was true, she was at a clinic in a small town in the Black Forest. That's when the hooting started and he shut the window on me. But that's not all, Paula. I had a good look inside the mini, and there was nothing there."

James paused again, this time with dramatic effect.

"What do you mean, nothing there?" asked Paula obligingly.

"Oh, there was a road atlas and a few things like that lying on the seat beside him, but nothing at all on the back seat or on the floor. Don't you find that odd?"

"I expect his luggage was locked up in the back," said Paula. "Not everyone is as untidy as I am."

"Well, I found it very odd indeed," said James stubbornly. "One always has something or other in the car if one is going a long way, especially abroad. Thermos and sandwiches. Overnight case. Some sort of briefcase if one is carrying papers. And if there really is an old lady in a nursing home, he'd be taking her something or other. There ought to have been all sorts of bits and pieces in the car."

Paula, whose thoughts had been wandering again, gave him her full attention and decided that he was right.

"It all points to the conclusion that there isn't an old lady novelist at all," she said. "The house is a fake, and he's not going to visit anyone in a nursing home, either here or in the Black Forest. It looks very much as if he's just running away. But who tipped him off? Was it my phone call yesterday? Or the literary agent? Or even Caroline Martyr—she might be more involved than we know. But surely it couldn't be George Bruce." Paula became excited. "I've got to talk to George Bruce, James. Let's get back to London. Quick."

"Don't you think it might be a good idea to have a closer look at High Beechwoods?"

"You mean the housekeeper may have returned," said Paula, "and we might learn more from her than we did from Robin Key? Well, I suppose that's possible," she continued as James made no reply, "but if she isn't there, we'll have wasted our time."

"Not necessarily," said James.

"But we couldn't get in."

"We could try," said James.

Paula stared at him. "Housebreaking as well as carchasing." She sighed. "Whatever next?"

But nevertheless she found herself agreeing to this preposterous suggestion. It really did seem as if she had taken leave of her normal sense of responsibility.

8

The black cat came from under the hedge to greet them when they got out of the car, and remained, this time, to make friends.

"Even if it doesn't belong here," said Paula, "it's expecting a welcome. But not from Robin Key. The housekeeper maybe."

"Who spoke on the phone with a heavy foreign accent?"

"I'm wondering if that was assumed," said Paula. "It might even have been Robin Key himself."

"What about the Rosie O'Grady who called at the publisher's and the agent's a few years ago?"

"Heavy scent, thick furs," said Paula thoughtfully. "No, I don't think that could have been Robin Key, although it might well have been a man. After all, George Bruce has met Robin Key and would surely have recognized him even in disguise. And I believe George was telling the truth about that visit, even if about nothing else. No. There's somebody else involved. Not a genuine, aging Rosie, but someone who lives in this house or who regularly comes here."

Paula bent down again. "I think it's a woman, and she likes cats," she added.

"Then let's confront her," said James, moving towards the front door and ringing the bell. They waited for some time and then he tried again. "There's no one here. I didn't think there would be. What now?"

"We'll follow the cat. She'll know the way in if there is one."

The black cat, who had been waiting patiently on the door-step to be let in, gave a disappointed mew and trotted off round the far side of the house. James and Paula, coming up close behind, saw a small casement window, a few inches open. The cat leapt up onto the window-sill and squeezed through the aperture. Paula peered through after it.

"It's a sort of utility room," she said. "And I think I can— yes, I'm sure I can! This is the first time I've ever been glad to be small."

She felt inside and released the catch of the window so that it opened to its full width. "If you could sort of push me through the window as if I was a parcel," she said, "but I'd like to land feet first, please."

It would have been impossible for her to manage the manoeuvre on her own, but together they contrived an awkward piece of ballet that ended with Paula standing unharmed on the bare wooden floor of a small room containing a washing-machine and a dryer and some cupboards.

"Can you open the door?" asked James, leaning on the window-sill from outside and looking around with interest.

Paula hoped so. It would be much more difficult for them to get her out through the window than it had been to get her in. The cat had found a saucer with milk in it and was lapping eagerly. It had taken no notice of Paula's unorthodox entry, but became very interested when she pulled open the door.

Here was the kitchen, tidy, well equipped, but apart from an empty milk bottle standing in the sink, showing no signs of recent use. The cat began a routine examination of everything at floor level and Paula went to the outer door, turned the big old-fashioned key, and called to James to come in.

"It's all too easy," he said. "If there is a housekeeper living here, I don't believe she's gone away. She's probably shopping or something."

"I quite agree, and she could be back any moment. We'll have to hurry."

"What are we looking for?"

"Any sign whatever of genuine habitation. Any clues to the nature of the inhabitants. I'll take the bedrooms, you do the living-room."

They wasted no more time nor words. The two bedrooms were of medium size and had as much the appearance of a show-house as did the living-room.

The bungalow was carpeted throughout in the same pale

grey, but one of the bedrooms had yellow draperies and the other had blue. In the blue bedroom there was a man's rain-coat hanging in the fitted cupboard and a pair of rubber boots on the floor. Otherwise the drawers and cupboards were empty. In the yellow bedroom there were signs of occupation. The wardrobe contained a selection of women's clothes, of average size and sober in tone, but all of expensive make.

Paula had the impression of a middle-aged or elderly woman who was not particularly interested in clothes but who liked to have really good things. She opened drawers, feeling sickened with herself, for along with her own curiosity about her fellow human beings went strong feelings about the sanc-tity of personal privacy. She had to tell herself firmly that the circumstances were exceptional, that here was a mystery, possibly even a crime, to be uncovered, before she could bring herself to look closely at the contents of the drawers.

The clothes and the very few cosmetics were in keeping with the rest of the possessions. Certainly not a vain woman, but equally certainly not one who completely neglected her appearance. And whoever used this room, whether perma-nently or only occasionally, was most likely an English-woman, which meant that in all probability the telephone voice had been assumed.

On the bedside table, next to the reading-lamp, was a slim glass vase containing a single yellow rose. Some of its petals had fallen. Paula remembered the roses in the living-room and thought: This is genuine; this woman really likes to have flowers around her, and she is certainly going to be here again today, because she will want to change the roses for fresh ones, and she must have been here earlier because of the milk put out for the cat.

Were there any other clues about the sort of woman who used this room?

Paula picked up the two books lying on the bedside table. One of them was a paperback containing poems by John Betjeman, a choice that seemed to blend in well with the clothes. The other book was an old edition of *Jane Eyre*, in a red leather binding and with gold leaf round the edges.

To Paula this was instantly recognizable as a much-loved book, perhaps a relic of school-days.

Jane Eyre. Yes, this too was absolutely right. The basic

Rosie O'Grady story, transformed out of all recognition by the heart and mind of a genius. With great excitement Paula opened the book. It was a lovely edition: clear print on India paper. Attached to the inside of the front cover was a printed label headed "St. Mary's School, Seaford, Sussex," and stating that this book had been awarded as a prize for work of merit to "Joan Cook."

Joan Cook. The name was written in an old-fashioned copy-book hand with a long tail to the *J* and an upward flourish of the final *n* and the final *k*.

Paula stood still with the book open in her hands, momentarily forgetful of time and place, lost in a nostalgic reverie about the much-loved books of her childhood.

The sound of voices brought her back to the present. Hastily she replaced the two books where she had found them and ran to the door of the yellow bedroom. The voices came from the living-room the other side of the hall. One of them was James, apologizing with great energy.

"I'm most dreadfully ashamed. Of course it's a criminal offence. It's completely unforgivable . . . my friend and myself . . . no, we didn't break in. We found the back door unlocked. There was this nice little black cat, you see, and it was mewing outside the back door, and Paula and I—well, we're both cat people, and well, I'm afraid we just pushed at the door, and of course people do still leave their doors open in country places even nowadays, and of course we ought not to have come in but we did and here we are. Snooping. It's Rosie O'Grady's house, isn't it? Paula is doing a study of Rosie O'Grady's novels for George Bruce, the publisher. Ah— here she is . . ."

James in full flood of apology was not easy to interrupt. Paula had heard the woman's voice trying once or twice to break in, but without success.

"This is James Goff and I am Paula Glenning, both of the University of London," she said, coming forward into the room. "Miss O'Grady's publisher has commissioned me to write a study of her novels, and my colleague has been helping me. I need to know something about her life and character as well, and since nobody seems to know anything about her at all, I've been reduced to this sort of desperate measure."

"Very desperate," said the woman's voice gravely.

She looked to be in her early sixties, tall and slim, with a plain, sun-tanned face and thick straight grey hair. She was wearing a light-blue summer costume, very simple but very well cut, white leather shoes, and carried a handbag to match.

This was the woman of the yellow bedroom without a doubt. The *Jane Eyre* lover. Joan Cook.

"I had a letter of introduction from George Bruce to Mr. Key," went on Paula, "but Mr. Key has got it. I don't know whether you'd like to call George Bruce yourself. He would vouch for us."

"I've no doubt he would." The deep voice sounded faintly amused. "But I feel rather more inclined to call the police."

"You have every reason to do so," said James. "We are trespassers. We are entirely in your hands."

There was a short silence. The black cat roamed around the room and the newcomer stood near the desk, looking thoughtfully from one to the other of the intruders.

A plain face, thought Paula, but a strong one. Very intelligent. Not altogether unfriendly, but not particularly kindly or forgiving.

At last she spoke. "You are indeed guilty of a criminal offence, but I doubt if our local police force would be pleased to be called in on such a case. And as for George Bruce, I hardly need his confirmation of your identity, Mrs. Glenning. I very much admired your book about Mr. Goff's famous grandfather, but I don't think you did yourself justice in that television item. You were too modest."

"But I'm not modest," cried Paula indignantly. "I know I did a good job on that book."

"Then you must learn to project your personality more effectively. Whether or not you will have the opportunity of doing so over a study of Rosie O'Grady is something we will have to discuss."

"You aren't Rosie O'Grady yourself, then?" burst out James.

The woman laughed. "No. As Mrs. Glenning has no doubt discovered, my name is Joan Cook. I doubt if she has discovered anything else, and I doubt even more whether you have discovered anything at all, Mr. Goff."

"Nothing at all," said James, sadly shaking his head, but Paula, knowing him well, was not so sure. "So you aren't going to call the police?" he went on.

"Whether or not I make any charge against you depends on yourselves. I have had a rather exhausting day shopping and doing errands in Maidstone, and I'm going to make some coffee and sandwiches for all of us before I unpack the car. This will give you a chance to talk together and decide what to do. Come on, Kitty." Her voice softened as she addressed the black cat. "I've brought something very tasty for you."

The door of the living-room closed behind her. "It's no use our just walking out," said James, "because we can't get away until she moves her car. What d'you think she wants, Paula? What's the price of our being let off?"

He went on to answer his own question as Paula did not immediately reply. "Presumably we have to promise to abandon our researches."

"I'm not so sure," said Paula. "I don't think she knows herself what she's going to do. But she very much wants to know how much we have found out about Rosie. And we want to know what *she* knows, so it boils down to a question of which side puts its cards on the table first. And since we are very much in the wrong and she could make things unpleasant for us if she wanted to, I guess we're the ones who have to do the talking."

"How much do we tell her?"

Paula thought a moment. "Everything we've learned to date. We've nothing to lose, and we might even learn something new. We might even find she's an ally."

James agreed rather doubtfully. "But who the hell is she? And how did you know her name?"

Paula explained about the school-prize edition of *Jane Eyre*. "I've no idea who Joan Cook is," she went on, "except that I've got a very strong suspicion that she's written at least some of the O'Grady books. Listen, James, stripped of all the trimmings of the Brontë imaginative powers, what's the basic form of *Jane Eyre*?"

"Poor little orphan girl captures the heart of a rich man with a mysterious past. All she has is her honesty and her courage. And her virtue, of course. Good Lord."

"Yes," said Paula. "It's the Rosie O'Grady plot, isn't it?"

"Well, yes, but really, I mean, Brontë—and after all, you could take almost any great work of literature and strip it down into a Rosie O'Grady plot or something of that ilk. You might as well say that any cover girl is fundamentally the same as the Mona Lisa because they're both built on the same framework of the human skull. It's the treatment that matters, not the skeleton.''

"Of course, of course," cried Paula. "I'm not talking about aesthetic values, I'm talking about the feelings of individual human beings. Why does one have a favourite book? Why did you go to such lengths to acquire a first edition of *Huckleberry Finn*? Why am I hooked on Chekhov? I don't suppose any of us will ever understand our deepest dreams and yearnings.''

"Maybe *Jane Eyre* just reminds Joan Cook of her happy school-days," said James in a very matter-of-fact way. "If you want to link her with Robin Key's editor or co-author or whatever, then I should think the fact that she is here and very much in possession at High Beechwoods is far stronger evidence than any amount of literary theory.''

"Of course it is, but I do like things to feel psychologically right. Don't you think she had a hand in some of those books, James?''

"If she did, then why doesn't she come forward herself as Rosie O'Grady?''

"Because she likes her privacy. Because Robin Key has some hold over her and won't let her. Because she's not old enough to be the original Rosie and it would spoil the whole Mystery Lady publicity mystique if she turns out to be a series of people.''

"She's too young to be old Mrs. Martyr's Rosie who went to Canada," said James, "but she is old enough to be the person who sent off that first manuscript from Railway Cottages in Brighton. Thirty-six years ago. Joan Cook would have been about eighteen or twenty.''

"But we haven't got anything at all to link her up with the Railway Cottages end," objected Paula.

"Not yet," agreed James.

Paula looked at him suspiciously. She was sitting on the settee near to the table where the bowl of fading roses stood. He was standing by the window, looking in her direction but with his face in shadow.

"James," she said in a low voice, "what did you find in this room?''

He made no reply.

"You've got something. You've taken something. You've got to put it back. We might get searched."

"Are you suggesting that I would descend to stealing a document from somebody else's house?" he said with a most convincing air of injured innocence.

"You certainly would. You've done it before," snapped Paula.

"But that was my own grandfather. And it was almost my own house. And you of all people have benefitted from it."

This last was only too true. Paula's study of James's famous grandfather would not have been possible if it had not been for some rather doubtful behaviour on the part of the grandson. She could not immediately think of a suitable retort, which was fortunate, because when Joan Cook came back into the room a moment later, the others gave the impression of having been silent for some time, and not of having just broken off a discussion.

James was still standing by the window and Paula was picking up some fallen rose petals and placing them in the big glass ashtray. We certainly don't look as if we have been concocting some lies, she thought, and perhaps it's just as well that I don't know what James has been up to.

She got to her feet. "Thank you very much indeed, Miss Cook, for giving us the opportunity to talk things over. I'd like to tell you straight away that George Bruce actually asked me to write a popular biography of Rosie O'Grady, and not just to write about the novels. He's paid me a big advance on royalties and given me unlimited expenses and a completely free hand. He wants something sensational, of course. Up till today I've been investigating in a perfectly legitimate manner, but not making any progress, and I was getting very frustrated. That's no excuse for intruding into your home, but if you would like me to tell you exactly what I have discovered, then I will do so now, and after that you can decide what to do with us."

"Thank you," said the grey-haired woman, inclining her head slightly. "That's what I had hoped you would say."

9

"That's all, I think," said Paula after she had been talking for some time with no interruptions from James and only an occasional question from Joan Cook. "When you came in, I'd just found your copy of *Jane Eyre* on the bedside table and had looked inside and seen your name. Otherwise I'd only formed general impressions."

"And Mr. Goff?"

Joan Cook turned to James with a look of inquiry.

"I didn't get much further than general impressions," he said. "What I was looking for in here was some evidence of a writer's study—something to show that creative work actually went on here. Bits of torn-up manuscript in the waste-paper basket, sheets of typescript with corrections. That sort of thing. And I found nothing. Of course I tried the drawers of the desk and found them locked," he added with a rueful smile.

Joan Cook looked at him thoughtfully, and Paula waited anxiously for her reaction. More and more was she convinced that James had made some discovery, and having been completely honest herself, she was now afraid that she might unwittingly give him away. Paula had often accused James of believing that he was good-looking and charming enough to get away with anything, but on this occasion she actually found herself hoping that he would succeed.

At last Joan Cook spoke. "I am grateful to you for being so open with me, and for telling me a number of things that I did not know myself. I have never heard of Mrs. Martyr and her granddaughter Caroline, and the O'Grady family of Railway Cottages in Brighton. All this has been a complete revelation to me, and I must ask you to be patient while I digest it."

Paula's relief that James was not under suspicion was lost in her surprise at this speech. How could anybody so very much at the heart of the mystery as Joan Cook appeared to be not know anything about the original Rosie? Could it possibly be that the Railway Cottages business was a completely false trail, that Mrs. Martyr's reminiscences had nothing to do with the Mystery Lady at all?

Joan Cook sat silent and still, stroking the black cat who now lay on her lap. James and Paula looked at each other in their puzzlement.

"How very extraordinary," said James. "Our story doesn't fit in with yours at all, then?"

"As far as I know, no," was the reply. "Are you absolutely sure that the first O'Grady manuscript came from the Brighton address?"

"The covering letter had that address on it," replied Paula, "and the letter from the literary agent saying he was interested in the book was sent to that address and obviously reached the author, so one has to assume that the manuscript was posted by somebody who had access to Number 2 Railway Cottages at the time, even if they were not actually living there."

"Yes, yes. We must assume that. But when I think that all these years—forgive me, Mrs. Glenning. This has been quite a shock to me."

"Would you like some more coffee?" said James, getting up again.

"Would you rather be alone?" asked Paula.

Joan Cook raised her head and smiled at them both. It lightened the rather heavy face and gave life to the grey eyes, her best feature.

"It was bound to happen one day," she said. "One cannot keep up a pretence for ever. I like you two in spite of your outrageous behaviour, and I am going to tell you my own story. But first of all I want to be quite sure that we are not interrupted. I must make a phone call. No, there's no need for you to leave the room."

A moment later she said into the telephone: "I'm at Forest Brook and shall stay here tonight and tomorrow. Any messages?"

She sat listening for what seemed to the others to be a very long time.

"I see," she said at last. "Yes, it was bound to happen one day. But we've been suspecting for some time that G.B. was going to do something of this sort. Do you think you've put them off the scent?"

Again she listened, looking straight at Paula, who saw that she was smiling again, and believed she could even detect a faint sign of a wink.

"Yes, they may very well suspect that you haven't really gone to Ostend," she said into the telephone, "but they won't have any idea where you are and they've no means of finding out. I don't see that we need take any action. Everything is perfectly in order here. If the telephone rings I follow the usual procedure. And the same applies if anyone comes to the door."

Yet again she listened.

"Persistent? Yes, it was rather persistent to follow you to Dover. They were exceptionally lucky not to lose you. It all sounds rather childish to me, but I don't see that there is any reason to be worried. After all, even if it does all come out, it doesn't really matter now. We're hardly in need of any more money, and I've been saying for a long time that I would like to retire. The last two books have been very poor. Yes, I know you don't want G.B. to publish a biography, and neither do I, but after all we've done nothing criminal. We'll live it down. It will be a seven-day wonder and soon forgotten, and you and I can go our separate ways and retire in peace with our hard-won gains. . . .

"All right, then, we will talk it over. Not tonight. You must be very tired of driving, and I certainly don't feel like any exhausting discussions today. Tomorrow? All right. I'll be here."

She replaced the receiver. "Poor Robin," she said, "he does get so agitated. Perhaps that was a bit mean of me, but from what you say, he has not played straight with me and I am not pleased."

"But where is he?" asked James. "Is he near here?"

"That, my dear Mr. Goff, is the one thing I am not going to tell you. I beg your pardon. I should have said one of the two things that I am not going to tell you. The other one is the address from which I lead my non-Rosie O'Grady life."

"So you really are the Mystery Lady," said Paula.

"One of them," corrected Joan. "Up till now I have been under the impression that the other, the original Rosie O'Grady, was Robin Key's wife, but your researches have produced yet a third one, going even further back."

"Old Mrs. Martyr's pretty milliner who went to Canada to have her illegitimate twins," said Paula. "I still can't help feeling that she is responsible for those early books, before the change of style. It's psychologically right, just as it's psychologically right that you should love *Jane Eyre* and be—well, what you are, and that you should have written the later books."

"And what am I?" inquired Joan.

Paula looked very embarrassed. "I'm terribly sorry. It's this wretched literary-critic habit one gets into in a job like mine. I've gone and let my tongue run away with me as usual."

"Yes, my dear, I know," said the older woman more kindly. "I used to be like that myself when I was reading English Literature at Oxford. I used to write essays making Olympian pronouncements about what George Eliot had in mind when she created Adam Bede or what Jane Austen's real feelings about poor unmarried ladies were. Do you think one can ever know what an author really has in mind?"

"No," said Paula. "I don't know why we keep trying."

"Excuse me, ladies," said James, "but do you think you could defer this discussion to another occasion? If Miss Cook is going to tell us how she became Rosie O'Grady, which is the last thing we deserve after what we have done, then—"

"—why doesn't she hurry up and get on with it," concluded Joan Cook with a smile. "Paula—I may call you Paula?—and I will talk about literature another time. Robin Key? No. We will start with myself. I'll make it brief. Born during the First World War. Only child, comfortable home in Sussex. Good education, always fond of writing stories. Oxford University degree. Good life on the whole, but too shy for close friendships. Parents killed in Second World War.

Very lonely time. Women's Air Force. Then the miracle. And after that the end of the world.''

She paused. The cat jumped down from her knee and walked over to Paula. James, after a quick glance at the older woman's face, turned his own away. There was something so sore and raw there, still, after all these years, that it was an intrusion to look at her.

"Got to know a Polish airman," continued Joan in the same jerky, breathless manner. "Conquered the shyness. Married him. We were happy. Only together when he had leave. Fighter pilot. Not very frequent leaves. We were happy. Killed just before peace was declared.''

There was a silence. At last she said in her normal voice: "That's my personal story. Now I will tell you how I became transformed into the final Rosie O'Grady.

"After my husband's death I came out of the Air Force and worked in various publishing houses for several years, at first as a secretary and gradually moving on to editorial work. In the early 1950s I was appointed as an editor in George Bruce's firm, and almost as soon as I took up the post there was great excitement about the latest Rosie O'Grady book.

"The manuscript was hopeless. William Broadway's office had worked on the earlier ones and made them tolerable but they'd given up on this. George called me into his office one day and said he was very pleased with my work and was hoping that I'd be able to help in this very important matter. He'd had a long talk with Robin Key, Miss O'Grady's manager, and the upshot was that Robin had promised to find somebody to work on the manuscript and on future manuscripts so that they could be submitted in something more approaching a publishable condition. 'There really are limits,' said George, 'even with this sort of money-spinner, and that script was way beyond the limit.' ''

"Robin Key told us this," put in James. "About the conference with George Bruce and its outcome.''

"He did? That was honest, at any rate. Now enters Joan Cook. Except that I was not known as Joan Cook, of course, when I was working with George Bruce, but by my Polish name, which is something else that I don't propose to tell you. George was becoming very worried when he sent for me, because two months had passed and there had been no word from Robin about the manuscript, nor indeed about anything else. It looked as if Robin was having great difficulty finding anybody to do the job, and George was beginning to have regrets. Maybe we could have done it in the office after all, maybe if he'd known how good I was at the editing work. And so on.

"But even at that time there was some sort of mystery about Rosie O'Grady. Nobody in the office, not even George, had ever seen her, and after the first book, all correspondence had been through Robin. Nobody knew that she was his wife. Well, maybe she wasn't, but that's what he told me, and what I have believed all these years.

"All that George Bruce knew was that she wanted no publicity, and being George, he decided to make a virtue of necessity and capitalize on this very fact. Hence the Mystery Lady business, which went down very well on the whole, but sometimes provoked the wrong sort of rumour.

"George felt very strongly that he himself, even if nobody else in the firm, ought to know exactly who and what she was, and I could see his point. The reason for my own summons to his presence was that he wanted me to undertake a mission, to kill several birds with one stone. I was to come down here and call on Robin Key myself, unannounced, but with a letter of introduction to vouch for my bona fides, and the way I conducted my mission was entirely up to me. The most important thing was, of course, to try to ensure that there would be a further supply of books by Rosie O'Grady. If Robin had found no one to work on them, then I was to suggest that I do it myself. In particular, I was to bring back the rejected manuscript, in whatever condition, so that I could put it in order.

"This was top priority, but almost as important, in George's view, was that I should find out something more about Rosie herself. See her, talk to her, get some sort of impression. Not for publicity. George was keeping faithfully to that promise, but to satisfy his own curiosity and his own quite justifiable concern. For a publisher does like to know something about the age and prospects and state of health of his top-selling authors. That's only right. After all, he's making an investment in them, and you wouldn't invest in anything if you knew it was going to collapse tomorrow. Would you, James?''

''No indeed, but I'm afraid an awful lot of people will persist in regarding publishing as a charity rather than as a business. Although, of course, risks must be taken,'' he added hastily, seeing a rather reproachful look on Paula's face, ''where the work is really worth while.''

''Exactly,'' said Joan, ''and I'm labouring this point because I do firmly believe that George's motives in sending me on this mission were quite reasonable and legitimate. He couldn't possibly have foreseen what it could lead to, and in one sense it caused him a great deal of worry and anxiety, although in the long run he was the gainer by a series of O'Grady manuscripts.''

''The detective!'' exclaimed Paula suddenly. ''You were the detective!''

''I was certainly expected to do some detecting,'' said Joan.

''I forgot to tell you,'' said Paula. ''I didn't mean to leave anything out, but it slipped my mind. The literary agent's secretary told me that George once put a detective onto Rosie but that it came to nothing. He never told me himself, and became evasive when I challenged him with it. I thought this was because something awful had happened to the detective— wild dogs, all sorts of Gothic horrors came to my mind.''

''On the contrary,'' said Joan. ''When I first came to High Beechwoods and explained that I was to work on the manuscript myself if a suitable editor had not been found, I was received most courteously. More than that. With great warmth. I did not know then, of course, that I was about to take a decision that was to lead to a sort of living death.''

10

The shadows were lengthening on the lawn; the black cat had asked to be let out and was stalking something in the long grass at the far end of the garden; Joan produced cigarettes and sherry and continued with her narration.

"Why did I agree to disappear completely as Mrs. Joan so-and-so and start another life as Miss Joan Cook, but keeping right away from anybody who had ever known me in that capacity before? Not only that, but to act the part of the aging author, Miss Rosie O'Grady, on the very few occasions when it was absolutely essential that a living human being should be made visible or audible?

"Why did I? Do you know what I mean"—and she turned to Paula—"when I say that it was a sort of living death?"

"No, I don't think I understand," replied Paula. "Do you mean that you lost the sense of personal identity? That you were living in the characters in your books?"

"It might have been that," said Joan, looking at Paula without seeing her. "But I wasn't exactly happy in my own identity. Perhaps that's why I gave in so easily to the temptation to lose it. At any rate," she continued more briskly, "it was a very lonely business, but it was partly my own fault. I do have a home, you know, apart from High Beechwoods. A very pretty period cottage in a pretty village. I go to church sometimes and take some part in village activities. I could do much more, but I don't want to. I'm an unsociable person and I make the excuse that it would be unwise to get too friendly with anyone. Besides, I would only be playing a

73

part. Not being myself. Although I hardly know any longer what 'myself' really is, so perhaps that ought not to matter.''

She crushed out her cigarette and turned from one to the other.

''Ought I to have done it? Have I done wrong? Have I injured anyone by agreeing to this pretence? I feel so guilty. All the time. But surely I have done no harm. Have I, James? Have I, Paula?''

They tumbled over each other in their eagerness to reassure her. No, of course she had done no harm. Just think of all those millions of people all over the world who had gained such pleasure and comfort from her novels. How could she possibly have done any harm?

''Perhaps you are right.'' She passed a hand over her eyes. ''It is very strange to be talking openly like this. I never thought to speak with honesty to any human being again. Well, I must get on with my tale or James will be getting impatient. Now we come to Robin Key. You don't feel very favourably disposed towards him at the moment, no more than he feels towards you, but I must ask you to forget that and to try to imagine him thirty years ago, in his forties.

''He was never good-looking but he had dignity and intelligence. He told me that he had worked at a number of different jobs, and for the last few years had been a publisher's representative, selling books, and that it had been his ambition to start his own bookshop. In one of the shops he visited he had met Rosie O'Grady, had encouraged her to write, and had undertaken to try to sell her efforts.

''That was the beginning of the partnership between them. The books did so well that he was able to give up his job and devote himself full-time to helping her with the writing, doing research for her, dealing with all the financial side. They got married, bought this house, and for the next few years all went smoothly.

''Their only serious problem was Rosie's health. She had always had very bad coughing fits and it was diagnosed as tuberculosis. In those days—not long after the end of the war—it was still a killer. One forgets how recent some of the wonderful advances in medicine have been. Her last manuscript was written when she was already very ill. Robin didn't say anything about this to George when they had their long conference. I told him that he should have told George, and he said yes, he knew, but he couldn't bring himself to speak of it. He was still trying to persuade himself that Rosie would recover.''

"I believed that his feelings for her were very strong. I still believe this, even though, if your story is true, much of what he told me must have been lies. But I will continue with what he told me, which is what I believed, without any suspicions, until I met you today.

"Rosie had died ten days before my visit. In a sanatorium in Switzerland, where she spent the last weeks of her life. Robin had been with her at the end and had stayed on to arrange the funeral. It was very quiet, just as she would have wished. A cousin had come over from Ireland, but otherwise only Robin and the priest and a couple of nurses from the sanatorium.

"He returned to High Beechwoods completely desolate and in no state to worry about the unsatisfactory manuscript. Of course I could only feel pity for him. I listened to him talking about Rosie and asked to see a photograph. He said he had gone quite crazy when he got back and destroyed all those he had, but now regretted it. He could not bring himself to dispose of her possessions, though, and he showed me her clothes and asked me what he should do with them. All the time he was saying that this was her favourite dress, or that she always liked to wear red. That sort of thing.

"I had explained my errand as soon as I came into the house, but it was a long time before we began to speak of it. When at last we did, he seemed quite at a loss. He couldn't cope with the manuscript himself and he couldn't possibly find anyone to lick it into shape. And in any case, Rosie O'Grady was dead, so there wouldn't be any more books. We agreed that this was a pity, from many points of view.

"He made me coffee and sandwiches, just as I did for you. I had great difficulty in getting here, by the way. There was a very infrequent bus service that stopped about a mile from the village, and I had to walk that, and then walk on up the hill and along the track, and had no idea how I was going to get back to London. It was late afternoon and raining hard. He suggested I should stay the night, and I knew I could trust him not to make a nuisance of himself. I don't quite know why, but there was between us, from the very first, a sort of respect, a sort of distance—I don't know how to describe it. Neither of us was the least bit attracted to the other, but each had the feeling of being needed by the other, of being able to help.

"I think that's what tipped the balance. The feeling that I was needed. Personally as well as professionally, but at the same time with no emotional commitment."

"Excuse me a moment," interrupted Paula at this point, "but could you tell us how the bungalow was furnished and decorated at that time?"

"It had a feeling of a lived-in house," replied Joan. "Rather tasteless, not very elegant, but warm and snug. A wood fire in here and chintzy furnishings. The garden was overcrowded too, like an old-fashioned cottage garden. And Robin used to like cats then. The tabby down at the farm was always visiting."

"When did you change it all?" asked Paula.

"About two years after we had gone into partnership, when we decided to buy houses for ourselves elsewhere and to use this place primarily as a mailing address and as something to show if it ever needed to be proved that Rosie O'Grady had an existence and a home. We never let it remain unvisited for more than a very few days at a time. One or the other of us would come and remain for a day or two. Sometimes longer."

"And there is no housekeeper?"

"Nobody. Robin or I would put on an act if necessary. We are both quite good mimics. We had routines worked out for any contingency, including actually appearing in front of George Bruce in person. That was risky, but it needed to be done, and it was done successfully."

"I'm sorry," said Paula. "I think I interrupted you. You were about to explain how the idea of carrying on with the novels as if the author were still alive came about."

"Yes, it was when we were looking at her last manuscript after breakfast the next morning. It was Saturday, and I'd nowhere to go back to except my bed-sitting-room in North London and nothing in particular to do.

"I liked it here. I'd slept well and explored the garden and the woods and made friends with the tabby cat. I'd even waved to one of the men at the farm from a distance, but Robin didn't encourage that. Don't quarrel with neighbours, he said, but no need to be chatty. Apparently Rosie never talked to them at all and never went into the village. They drove to Maidstone to shop. And the farm changed hands soon after she died and we've barely seen the people who live there now. They've no idea that this is the address of a very well-known author and they don't even know our names.

"But I'm wandering again. Back to that fatal morning, sitting in this room discussing the manuscript."

"The wartime one," said Paula.

"That's right. We went through it together, page by page, and I seemed to be inspired. Dramatic moments, snatches of dialogue, twists and turns of plot—all sprang into my mind as if some unseen being was prompting me. As if the spirit of Rosie was taking me over.

"Robin was amazed. 'You're as good as she was,' he kept saying, 'you're even better than she was. You've got to write. You've simply got to.'

"I said that I should like to, but I didn't think any publisher would accept me. He agreed that it was very difficult indeed to get started, but that Rosie had managed it. And I remember my very next words, and exactly where we were sitting when I said them.

"I said: 'If I rewrote this book completely and sent it to a publisher as the work of Rosie O'Grady, they would be delighted and it would sell many thousands of copies. If I sent in exactly the same manuscript under my own name, they would turn it down, or, if somebody did publish it, it would hardly sell at all. That's the way it is.'

" 'Then the obvious thing to do,' said Robin, 'is for you to send it in as the work of Rosie O'Grady. And there's no reason why you shouldn't send in the next one too.'

" 'But Rosie is dead,' I objected.

" 'Nobody knows that except myself,' he replied, 'and a few other people none of whom knew her as Rosie O'Grady, but only as Rosamund Key.'

" 'What about the Irish cousin who came to the funeral?' I asked.

" 'The Irish cousin who came to the funeral doesn't know that Rosie ever wrote a book,' he replied. 'There's no question of linking her up with the best-selling novelist.'

"I still felt uneasy. It seemed to me that we would be committing some crime, but I honestly could not see quite what. The name was a pen-name in any case. The author had never appeared in public. There was no impersonation involved at that stage, and there was never any question of obtaining money under false pretences. As for the readers, it didn't matter who was writing the books as long as they were what was expected, and as far as the agent and the publisher were concerned, they had a healthy youngish Joan Cook to supply their product instead of an ailing Rosamund Key."

"I can't see that you've done any injury to anybody at all, except perhaps to yourself," said James. "But since we can't know what your life would have been like if you hadn't taken on the job of being Rosie O'Grady, there's no means of judging that either. How did you manage to disappear? That must have presented some difficulties. Didn't anybody try to trace you?"

"They did," admitted Joan. "More people than I would have expected to do so actually took an interest in me. George went so far as to put the police onto it. He felt guilty, you see. He probably thought I could have got myself murdered for some reason or other and that it was his fault. Poor George. I had to go abroad for a while, but it all died down eventually. I don't think there's any need to burden you with the mechanics of my transformation, nor with the details of our partnership over all these years. I have to confess that I have found it very irksome lately, and so has Robin. We are both growing old, and my inspiration has gone. There won't be any more books. I think we've both of us been wishing for some time that we could kill off Rosie O'Grady, but haven't quite known how to do it."

"It looks as if you will have to do it now," said Paula. "I'm afraid we've forced you to. But what will Robin say when he learns that you've broken trust after all this time?"

"I don't know. Perhaps I won't tell him. But that would mean more lies and I can't be bothered with them. I'm sick of pretence. I'll think about it tonight."

"But, Joan," said James, "if Paula is going to make use of what you've told her when she writes the life of Rosie O'Grady, then Robin will have to know."

"Paula can't write the life of Rosie O'Grady," said Joan,

"because she's only got half the story. Or rather, she has got two halves but they don't link up. How is she going to find the missing link?"

"I'm not going to find it because I'm not going to look for it," said Paula. "I shall tell George Bruce that I'm giving up the job and will be paying back the advance. I shall tell him that I've found out enough to know that the life can never be written."

James began to protest. "I've made up my mind," said Paula, "that as far as I am concerned, this inquiry is now at an end. All I care about is that Joan should be free to live how and where she wants. And that she should forgive us."

"Nothing to forgive," said the older woman. "It had to happen one day. It's been a relief to talk to you. And now I am going to ask your advice. In spite of my rude remarks about literary critics, I do believe they have something useful to say. You know the sort of novels that I have been writing for the last thirty years. I am now not far off seventy. What chances have I got of making a new career as a different sort of writer?"

Paula made no reply.

"That's the answer, I think," said Joan. "No chance at all."

"People do sometimes change their style very late in their career," said Paula doubtfully. "If you were freed from the strait-jacket of being Rosie O'Grady—"

"A strait-jacket? Perhaps. Or was it a vital prop?"

Joan sat brooding for a moment or two, and then said, "I'm inclined to think there is no future for Joan Cook as a writer of fiction. But as a biographer—that's not impossible. Suppose I take over your researches for you, Paula? I am very intrigued by the missing link, and I should think my chances of finding it are somewhat greater than yours."

"You would ask Robin Key? You would ask him straight out?" Paula could not keep the alarm out of her voice.

"Yes, I think so. He owes me an explanation."

"But if, I mean, suppose he—"

"Suppose that the reason for his lying to me was to conceal some disgraceful action of his own? Is that what you were thinking?"

"Yes," said Paula unhappily.

"That's what I am thinking too. It seems the obvious reason for his deception. On the other hand, it may be something quite trivial. When I was young, people used to go to great lengths to conceal the fact of illegitimacy. Nowadays nobody cares. But Robin is of the same generation as myself. It may be quite innocent or it may not be. In either case, I have got to know. This is my responsibility and nobody else's.'' She turned to James, who had made some sound of concern.

"You were only supposed to be writing my life, not living it for me,'' she said sharply.

He recoiled as if he had received a blow, and Joan stretched out a hand and touched his sleeve. "Ah!—don't be offended. I am not resentful. I did resent the manner of your intrusion— how could I not resent it?—but now my chief feeling towards you both is one of gratitude. I have talked so much. It shows how badly I needed to talk, that it should boil over like this. I needed to talk and I found you here, and you were the right people to talk to. Wasn't that lucky? Wasn't that fate?''

"I rather think it was George Bruce,'' muttered James.

"Of course it was George. He sent me here and it changed my life, and now he has sent you here and it has changed it again.''

She stood up. "I'll have to come and move my car so that you can drive yours out. It's very late. You'll be wanting to get back to London.''

They followed her to the front door. The lights from the living-room shone on the lawn; the beech trees were black against the indigo sky.

"Don't you feel lonely here?'' asked James.

"Lonely? Of course. But nothing like as lonely as I feel in the middle of my pretty village.''

"Are you sure you'll be all right? We can't help feeling worried about you, although, as you say, we've no right to.''

"You poor things. Yes, I can see you're worried. Now what can we do to make you less so?''

She led the way towards the front gate. When they had rearranged the cars and James was seated at the wheel of the Rover, she came and stood by its open window.

"Are you free the day after tomorrow?'' she asked.

James turned to Paula, who nodded.

"And you wouldn't mind the drive again? Then why don't

you come and hear the result of my inquiries? Come about four. Come to tea. This is a proper invitation.''

''Properly and gratefully accepted,'' said James. ''Thank you very much indeed. That would be lovely.''

''I shall look forward to it. And, Paula—'' Joan bent forward so that she could see into the car.

''Yes?'' Paula leant forward too.

''Don't tell George that you're giving up the job. Do you mind? Not till we've talked about it again.''

''I'd rather get it over with at once,'' said Paula.

''Yes, I know. But just till the day after tomorrow. Please. Please promise me.''

''All right then. And you will take care, won't you?''

''I'll take care. See you soon. Drive safely, James.''

11

In the village of Forest Brook there was no sign of life and very few lights in the houses. They came out onto a wider road, winding gently between high hedges, and almost clear of traffic at this time of night. The lights of the Rover shone far ahead, picking out the grass verge and the road surface.

Paula stared through the windscreen, half-hypnotized by the moving yet never-changing scene.

After a few miles she said, "Are you very tired, James? Is it any use my offering to drive?"

"Sorry, love. No. This car's too big for you. You'd better buy that mini you saw at Hampstead Motors."

"Will you come and look at it tomorrow morning? I'd like your opinion before I make an offer."

For a little while they talked about cars, and then fell silent again.

"I can't stop thinking about Joan," said James suddenly. "Wasn't Charlotte Brontë terribly lonely too?"

"I believe so. That's why she married. Pity."

"That she married or that she was lonely?"

"Both."

A few miles farther on James said, "You can't have it both ways."

"Have what?" asked Paula drowsily. She had been almost asleep.

"Never mind. Forget it," said James.

Where the motorway merged into another one they came into a great glare of lights and Paula woke up.

"Can you listen for a minute or two?" asked James.

"Yes. Sorry. Go ahead."

"I did find something out when I was snooping. You were quite right. It's probably of no importance, and if you're really going to give up the job it doesn't matter in any case, but I thought you'd like to know."

"Of course I want to know. It's just that—oh, James, I do wish with all my heart we'd never gone there."

"So do I. God knows what sort of Pandora's box we've opened up. But it had to happen one day, as Joan said herself. It was fate. Or George Bruce. Anyway, I didn't actually remove any document from the house. If I had, I really think I'd have had to confess, with all this soul-searching going on. It was while I was looking at the first hardback editions of the early O'Grady books. I picked one of them out and read what was written inside the front cover."

He paused a moment. "It said, 'To Robin, with all my love and thanks, from Eileen.' "

"From Eileen," repeated Paula. "What sort of handwriting was it?"

"Round and backward-sloping. What we intellectual snobs would call an uneducated hand."

"And did you see how many of the books were inscribed like this?"

"Just the first four. The next one—after the change—was not inscribed at all."

"That would be the wartime one," said Paula. "The manuscript that Joan salvaged and that started her career as Rosie O'Grady. Eileen. But according to Joan, Robin's wife was called Rosamund."

"Perhaps she was Eileen Rosamund. Or vice versa."

"Eileen O'Grady sounds possible," said Paula. "Did Mrs. Martyr ever say the name when we were in Brighton?"

"I've been trying to remember. I'm almost sure she didn't. But I could ask Caroline if it means anything to her."

"You might do that," said Paula. "I wonder if Joan has ever looked inside these books."

"More than likely. And she probably knows that Robin's wife was Eileen Rosamund. And if she knew about my discovery, she would know that it is trivial."

"I'm not so sure that it is trivial," said Paula. "I've got a hunch that it might even be the missing link. The Canadian twin. Or the O'Grady niece who took over the house. It's got to be one or the other of them, hasn't it, James?''

He laughed. ''Or one and the same person. Didn't I hear somebody say a little while ago that she was going to abandon the whole inquiry?''

''I'm not going to write a book,'' said Paula, ''but I can't help niggling away at it. Why do you think she invited us back?''

''Because she wanted to cancel out our intrusion by a formal invitation. Because she knows we are bursting with curiosity and is kind enough to satisfy it. Because she likes us. I don't know. Take your choice. The thing that puzzles me most is that she never had any suspicion that Robin was not telling her the truth. How could one work so closely with someone and never suspect?''

''It does seem to happen. Wives who discover after thirty years that their husbands have always been unfaithful. Or the other way round. We wouldn't have suspected anything about Robin if we'd heard Joan's story first, without knowing anything about the Brighton end. But when you do once know something, it's terribly hard to imagine what it's like not to know it.''

''The Garden of Eden. The eating of the Tree of Knowledge. Try not to worry about Joan, love. She made it very plain that she decides for herself and that we are to keep out. A very formidable lady. She got her own back on us, didn't she? Both you and me. 'I used to write that sort of thing when I was an undergraduate at Oxford.' '' James chuckled. ''Poor Paula.''

''Serves me right for taking on this snooping job. James, how on earth am I ever going to get clear of George Bruce?''

''No way. Never. Not now he knows you can write the stuff that brings in the money. You've got a life sentence. Like Rosie herself.''

It seemed a very fitting comment on the events of the day. The following morning Paula received a telephone call from George Bruce himself, asking how she was getting on with the Mystery Lady project. She replied cautiously that some progress had been made but that she would rather not say any more at this moment.

''That's great,'' said George. ''Keep at it. And keep in touch.''

He rang off. Paula felt sure that he had only called to find out whether she was alive and well.

"He's afraid I could disappear, like Joan," she said to James when they met to consider the purchase of the yellow mini-car.

James made uncomplimentary noises about George Bruce. "I had a phone call too," he added. "But first things first. Tell you about it later."

They drove three times across Hampstead Heath and back: the salesman full of chat and confidence; James full of complaints because the car was too small for him; and lastly Paula, nervous at first but gradually becoming happier.

The car was approved and the necessary bits of paper were exchanged.

"If you'd like some driving practice," said James when they were alone, "we could go to Brighton again. It was Caroline Martyr who called me this morning. But if you're really giving up the investigation—"

"I'm not going to write any book," said Paula.

"Then we'll have to look on it as doing research work for Joan. I'm sure she'd approve of our chasing up the Brighton end of the missing link. We got Caroline really interested, and she had a day off yesterday and went down to see her granny. Found the old lady much more amenable and was actually permitted to do some shopping and get her a meal. Caroline thanked me because she thinks it's because of our visit. So maybe we have done a bit of good with our blundering about, Paula."

"You certainly made a very generous donation to the preservation society."

"Oh yes, there's good news on that front too. Caroline says there's going to be yet another inquiry. They'll probably pull the cottages down in the end, but it could well hold it up for long enough to see Mrs. Martyr out."

"Let's hope so. What else did Caroline say?"

"That her grandmother didn't tell us the whole story," replied James. "She kept something back as a matter of principle."

" Or because she was hoping to receive another visit from that nice young man, James Goff," said Paula laughing. "Let's go. It's very noble of you to offer to be driven. The sacrifices you are making in the cause of solving the mystery of Rosie O'Grady!"

They were parked in a comparatively quiet street near the Heath, and she looked at him inquiringly before starting the engine.

"It's taking an awful lot of your time, James. This will be

the best part of another day. And there's High Beechwoods again tomorrow.''

"But I'm enjoying it," he replied so simply and openly that there was nothing more to be said.

The drive to the coast was uneventful, and when they were a couple of blocks away from Railway Cottages, Paula stopped the car.

"I'm going to park here and have a walk by the sea," she said. "You'll do better on your own."

He looked disappointed. "I'd much rather you were there."

"But she would not. Mrs. Martyr doesn't like women."

James had to admit that Caroline had hinted at this as well. "Despises them if they are feeble and resents them if they are not," he said. "A lot of women of that generation seem to have the same attitude. But not my grandma. She was very fond of you, Paula."

"And I of her. How long are you likely to be? Shall we meet here in an hour?"

After they had parted, Paula strolled down to the sea front and stood for a while watching the gulls hover and swoop at the entrance to the marina. Her thoughts were not with Rosie O'Grady, but with the Goff family. James had changed since his grandmother's death. It had been quiet and peaceful, unlike the death of her ex-husband, his famous grandfather, but in many ways it had affected him more deeply. He seemed to be less self-centered and more vulnerable than she had ever known him; and this had the curious result of making her feel more warmly disposed towards him but at the same time vaguely resentful.

One knows where one stands with thoroughly selfish people, she thought; they give a sort of structure to human relationships. You don't have to worry about them because they take care of themselves. But if somebody who used to be just such a prop turned out capable of feeling hurt and lonely himself, then it upset the balance.

Paula walked along in the direction of the pier and decided that she was a much more selfish person than James, because she could not endure the thought of any close personal commitment, of having any emotional demands made on her. It looked as if she and James were moving in different directions; that he was coming to terms with the need to give and take, and that she was becoming more and more uncompromising in her need for detachment. They were moving in different directions, and they had met on the way and would have to part again. And this time the parting would be entirely her own fault.

This train of thought was so depressing that Paula turned round, fearing another of the dark moods, and hurried back to where she had left the car. It had started to rain, a heavy summer storm, and it was a comfort to take shelter in the little yellow tin box that was now her own. She was not a very confident driver, and she would never have taken this step without James's encouragement.

For a man, power; for a woman, freedom. Somebody had once said that that was what it meant to acquire one's own car. Power in excess led to tyranny. Freedom in excess led to—no, not to license, but to loneliness. Like Joan Cook's loneliness. If that was what a life without personal ties was like, then no wonder most people clung to their relationships with others, however unsatisfactory. Paula found it painful to think of Joan, partly because she and James had behaved so badly, and partly because it seemed to be such a wasted life.

But suppose Joan had been the real Rosie from the first, a successful romantic novelist earning a lot of money and living in a big country house, shunning publicity, but with her own circle of friends and family.

One would hardly call that a wasted life. Why, then, was Joan so sad? Was it because of the pretence; or because of the absence of human contact; or because of her own past tragedy?

Paula was just deciding that nobody had any right to say that any life was wasted, whether one's own or somebody else's, when a rather wet James opened he passenger door and folded himself up inside the tiny car.

"Sorry," he said, "I'm dripping onto the seat."

"We can dry you out while we talk," said Paula. "Where's the heater?"

They drove along the coast road. The sun came out but the rain continued, and ahead of them, descending from just above the cliff-top in two clear arcs of colour to the deep-blue ocean, was a double rainbow. Paula pulled onto the grass verge and they sat there and stared at it, silent and fascinated.

After a minute it began to fade.

"If it was a photograph, you'd think it was faked," said James.

"I've never seen anything like it," said Paula.

They waited a little longer, half hoping that the glory would return, but the rain stopped and the sky cleared and the sky and sea and the grass on the cliff-top were bright in the sunshine but without any magic.

"Let's go in the direction of Forest Brook," said James presently. "I know we are not invited till tomorrow, but anyway, let's go."

After consulting the map, he went on, "Caroline was right. Mrs. Martyr didn't tell us the full story and she was hoping for another visit. She was very coy and it was really rather horrible and I've had to write another cheque for the preservation society, but at least I've found the missing link."

"Eileen?"

"Yes. Eileen O'Grady was the niece who found the old man dead. The last of the O'Gradys. You remember Caroline's story. Of course Mrs. Martyr knew about it, even though she wasn't living in Railway Cottages at the time. The old man was Walter. He was the eldest brother of the original Rosie O'Grady. The death was an accident. He was an alcoholic and so was his lady friend. Nobody ever questioned that it was accidental. Eileen had already been to see him once. She'd arrived on a ship from Montreal—"

"The twins!" cried Paula, taking her eyes off the road for a moment and hastily righting the mini in time to prevent it running into the hedge. "Rosie's illegitimate twins."

"It seems so." James hesitated.

"Go on, go *on*!" cried Paula. "Was Robin Key the other?"

"No. The other twin didn't survive. In any case, Robin Key is too young. I haven't got him sorted out yet, but I've got an idea. Two ideas. Paula, do you think we'd better stop awhile? No offence to your driving—you're doing fine, but it'll be easier to talk if we're stationary."

"This'll do," said Paula, turning into the yard of an expensive-looking and almost deserted road-house. "We can sit in the garden. I'll fetch our drinks. Please, James. You've spent so much time and effort on Rosie. Go and finish drying off in the sun."

She came back shortly with beer and sandwiches and they sat undisturbed, except for an occasional visit from an ancient black Labrador, while James explained his two ideas about Robin Key.

12

Not the drunken old Walter, but Eileen, his youngest sister's child, was the last of the O'Grady's. Mrs. Martyr was convinced of this. Of all that big family there was nobody left except this stranger from across the ocean who had papers to prove that she was indeed Rosie's daughter, papers good enough to satisfy the lawyers, at any rate.

So the house and all its contents were claimed by Eileen.

What sort of a woman was she?

Mrs. Martyr didn't think much of her, although in fact she had never met her. To start with, she was foreign, and that didn't go down well in Railway Cottages. But, even worse, she thought herself superior to them, in spite of being illegitimate, and she made it plain that she was going to get away from these low surroundings as soon as possible.

The neighbours who had known the O'Gradys in their best years were prepared to be friendly to the newcomer, and to talk to her about her relations; but the only thing that interested Eileen was how to get in touch with her natural father. This did not please Railway Cottages at all, because nobody, not even Rosie's own mother, had ever been able to find out who he was. Eileen also made it plain that if she did ever find him, she was certainly not going to let her mother's old neighbours know.

No, she certainly did not make herself popular, Eileen O'Grady from a little backwoods town in the province of Quebec, with her French phrases and her funny way of talking and her nylon stockings and her air of being so much

89

smarter than the shabby and war-worn residents of her mother's old home town.

In fact, she was really rather like her mother, with her grand ideas, except that Eileen, unlike Rosie, was not particularly pretty.

She was clever, though. That was evident in the way she handled the business of the house and its sale. She wasn't content to put it in the hands of the small firm that dealt in such modest properties; she went to one of the best estate dealers in the town and made such an impression on them that one of the young clerks actually came a number of times to the house. At least she said it was the estate agent's clerk, but it might well have been somebody else.

Whoever he was, he was surely hoping to get something out of it apart from a commission on the sale. There was money hidden in that house: Railway Cottages had always known it.

"So that," said James at this point in his narration, "is one of the candidates for Robin Key. The estate agent's clerk. We did think of it as a very outside chance when we were having lunch with Caroline, but I think he's now got to be considered a very good possibility."

"What firm was he working for?" asked Paula. "Oughtn't we to be back in Brighton making inquiries?"

"They no longer exist. Mrs. Martyr thinks they merged with another business but she doesn't know which one. We could find out, of course, and maybe we might find somebody who remembers something or could look up some records, but it could take a long time. This was about thirty-five years ago," concluded James on a rather defensive note.

"So you'd rather follow up the other possibility first," said Paula. "All right. This is your day for detective work and my day for driving. Who is the second candidate for Robin Key?"

"It's a wild idea," replied James as they walked back to the car. "It came to me when Mrs. Martyr told me the name of the place where her husband worked for that year as a gardener. She didn't tell us on our first visit, but then we never asked her. It was Willing Hall. Home of the Mountsey family. Does that mean anything to you?"

"Mountsey?" repeated Paula. "Not the poet Charles Mountsey?"

"The very same. Contemporary of my grandfather. Mrs. Martyr and I had quite a chat about it. The National Trust have got the house now, but when she and her husband were there, Charles Mountsey was still in residence, leading his hermit-like existence, with a succession of manservants trying to cope with him. Mrs. Martyr and her husband were fairly comfortable in the gardener's cottage, but it was much too much work for them, and Mountsey wouldn't pay them decent wages. He was a terrible miser, among all his other eccentricities. My granny met him once, before she ran away from Grandpa."

"But what is the link-up with Rosie O'Grady?" asked Paula as they drove away from the motel.

"Not Charles Mountsey himself, but the cousin from whom he inherited the estate," replied James. "Mrs. Martyr thought he was Eileen's father, although she didn't know for sure. The dates fit in, and there are a number of other local tie-ups. Now if Eileen came to England to find her father—"

"Money?" put in Paula.

"Or sentiment. Rosie, by this time, was dead. Anyway, Eileen knows, or soon finds out, where to go. Willing Hall in East Sussex. Where Mr. and Mrs. Martyr are living in one of the cottages. But Eileen goes straight to the house, and the person she sees is the man currently attempting to combine the jobs of librarian, secretary, estate manager, and valet to the famous mad poet Charles Mountsey. Mrs. Martyr says the general factotum would last on average three weeks. She lost track of those who came and went while she was there. There was a couple living in the other cottage who provided some sort of continuity and coped with the house and owner in between. They were the ones who found Charles Mountsey after he'd shot himself."

"Are they still alive?"

"I doubt it, but it's worth a try."

"So we are going to Willing Hall," said Paula.

"It's roughly in the same direction as Forest Brook. After we've been there—

"No prizes," said James a moment later, "for guessing who is my other candidate for Robin Key. He's obviously a resourceful and ingenious person. He's done a variety of different jobs. He's lived among upper-class society even if he comes from a different social background.''

"Mrs. Martyr didn't know who was working for Charles Mountsey at the time of Eileen's visit to Willing Hall?''

"She didn't actually tell me that Eileen had been there,'' admitted James, "and she got a bit confused at this stage. Or perhaps I got a bit confused. I'm sure she never met Eileen, but was simply repeating what she heard from neighbours when she returned to Railway Cottages. I did say this was rather a wild idea of mine. Maybe we ought to be going the round of Brighton estate agents after all.''

"They can wait,'' said Paula. "I'm looking forward to seeing Charles Mountsey's place.''

"We'll be there in about half an hour,'' said James.

They parked on the grass opposite the main entrance. There were only about twenty cars there, but space for many more.

"Not one of the more popular stately homes,'' said Paula, "but that may mean that someone will have time to talk to us.''

Just inside the main gate was a little hut that housed the pay desk and a selection of souvenirs. A tall white-haired woman sold them tickets, handed them forms of applications to join the Trust, and was happy to talk. Business was not brisk. They decided between the three of them that it always took some time before a recently acquired estate attracted a lot of visitors, and that Mountsey was not a widely read and popular writer.

"But an extraordinary personality,'' said James, "and I should have thought that the way he died—''

The white-haired woman did not like the idea of people visiting the house out of morbid curiosity. James hastened to remedy his mistake, and to identify himself as the descendant of an even more famous writer than the former owner of Willing Hall.

Paula left them to it, and wandered off to look at postcards and table-mats and books about wildlife, some of which would do for Christmas presents. Her thoughts had moved away from Rosie O'Grady when James came up to her and whispered, "The old couple are still here. Come on.''

They walked along a path between rhododendron bushes, all blossom long gone, dull-green in high summer.

"The house," said Paula. "It's over there."

There was a glimpse of grey stone behind the bushes. James pulled her into a side path. "Another time. The cottages are this way."

Paula resigned herself. After all, they were here for detective work, not for sightseeing.

"You see," said James, "it's most unlikely that the people living in the cottages would see anyone coming to the main door of the house. Unless they were actually working in that part of the grounds. So Eileen could have come here without anybody knowing except—"

"There ought to be a lodge," interrupted Paula.

"There used to be one at the gate, but it was in such a decrepit condition that the Trust pulled it down and put their shop there instead. Here we are."

He opened a small iron gate that led out of the main estate into a field path. On the left was ripening corn; on the right were vegetable gardens and two little thatched cottages.

"The first one," said James. "The other one is where Mr. and Mrs. Martyr lived when they were here. It's empty at the moment."

"Shall I come too? Wouldn't you do better alone?"

"You've got to come too," said James, "because you're supposed to be researching into Charles Mountsey. The lady at the gateway said you really ought to have written to the Area Offices and they would have fixed for somebody to meet you here, but I said that you wanted to get the feel of the place first."

"But I don't know anything about Charles Mountsey!" exclaimed Paula. "Only that he wrote rather Swinburne-like poetry and that he killed himself. I can't possibly talk to anyone about him."

"You don't need to know anything. You're not going to meet an expert. Only this old couple."

Paula still held back. "You didn't give my name, I hope?"

"No. I just said you were a colleague."

Paula was only partially placated. "Why didn't you say it was you who was researching on him?" she grumbled.

"Oh. I suppose I could have done that. But it doesn't matter. It got us the necessary information. Their name is Smith. Yes, honestly. And they've been here for ever and are very ancient. He seems to be quite spry, but she's in a wheelchair. Stroke. Paralysed. Can't speak much.''

Paula hung back again. ''They won't remember anything and I hate disturbing them.''

''Nonsense. They'll love it. We'll never be able to get away.''

James was right. Mr. and Mrs. Smith were delighted with the visit, and Mr. Smith more than made up for his wife's speechlessness. He came from the back of the house when they knocked on the door and took them into a small sitting-room, quite clean and tidy, but with an air of sickness about it. He was tall and upright, the sort of old man who remains the same for many years, but his wife was a white, wisp-like form shrouded in shawls and cushions. Occasionally she made a sound that he seemed able to interpret, and he assured them that her mind was perfectly clear and that she understood everything that was said.

James and Paula found this more distressing than if she had been sunk in a world of her own. To think and to see, but to be unable to take part in human contact or activity—surely this was the worst fate.

Mr. Smith talked a lot about Charles Mountsey and Paula found herself mentally storing facts. It was fascinating material. Perhaps she would read the poems and bring them into one of her seminars. That was, after all, the sort of thing she ought to be doing, trying to interest students in lesser-known English poetry. If George Bruce turned nasty when she told him she was finished with Rosie O'Grady, she could say that what she wanted to do was work on Charles Mountsey, a perfectly respectable subject for academic study.

Meanwhile Mr. Smith's tales flowed on, and James was trying to steer him towards the vital date: the summer of 1949.

Oh yes, he remembered that year. Two years after Mr. Charles moved in. Of course it wasn't like it had been when Mr. William had been alive, and here followed a long eulogy of William Mountsey, but it was nothing like as bad as it became later. At that time, said Mr. Smith, there was still somebody living in the other cottage who helped with the gardens, and he wasn't expected to do it all himself.

At this point Mrs. Smith made one of her unintelligible

noises and her husband turned to her and said, "That's right, my love. He wasn't much use, poor fellow. Invalided out of the army during the war, but he was better than nothing. Yes, I know you never got on with his wife and you were glad when they went, but I wasn't glad, because he was never replaced. After that it got worse and worse. Mr. Charles all alone up there at the house—wouldn't even let us in. Kept the door bolted and stared out at me from between the window curtains. We had to leave the milk and the other provisions on the doorstep and he fetched them in at dead of night— didn't he, Nell?—never saw him those last years. Only peeping out between the curtains, and then at the end. Oh dear me. That was bad. Very bad."

The old man shook his head.

"Skin and bones. Skin and bones. More dead than alive, I guess, even before he took up that gun. Skin and bones. And the state of the house—you wouldn't believe."

It had taken years to get the place into some sort of order, and the garden took even longer. Of course they had help by then—workmen all over the place—but it was never the same again. Not like when Mr. William was alive.

"I suppose there was a full staff up at the house then," said Paula. "A butler? A housekeeper?"

Mr. Smith allowed himself to be guided into discussing the indoor staff at Willing Hall and their rapid dispersal after Charles Mountsey came into residence. It was exactly as Mrs. Martyr had said. Charles trusted nobody, and nobody could endure his insane suspicions for long.

No, Mr. Smith could not remember much about any of the people who tried to cope with him. But the old butler now, in Mr. William's time—

James was beginning to look rather bemused, and Paula decided that it was time for a direct approach.

"In the summer of 1949," she said, "when the other cottage was still occupied, there was a woman came to visit Mr. Mountsey at Willing Hall. She wanted to see Mr. William, but she didn't know that he was dead. A Canadian woman. Do you remember her at all?"

"Canadian? No, I don't think—" began Mr. Smith, and was interrupted by another of the strange gurgling sounds from his wife.

He turned to her and a sort of communication, half-sound, half-gesture, passed between them.

Paula and James looked at each other and they, too, exchanged thoughts without speech. This is it, their glances said; in the clear mind of this paralysed old woman lies the vital clue.

"That's right, Nell," Mr. Smith was saying. "Now how could I have forgotten a thing like that?"

He turned back to James. "She's just reminded me," he said, "that that is the only time anybody ever got the better of Mr. Charles." He gave a wheezy little laugh. "This feller gave notice before he got the sack. Not like all the others."

He paused for several seconds, but neither James nor Paula dared to speak. It was Mrs. Smith who pushed her husband into further revelations. She was showing greater signs of animation than at any moment since the visitors had arrived. It was almost possible to imagine that the sound she uttered was "Go on, tell them."

"That's right. That was the one that walked out on Mr. Charles," said Mr. Smith. "Nothing much to look at. Quite a little chap. Face like a monkey. And clever as a monkey as well. Mrs. Smith and I always thought he went off with some of the silver, but nothing was ever done about it. Mr. Charles always believed he was being robbed, but he never knew what he'd got, so he never knew what he'd lost. And when he really was robbed—well, nothing was done. Yes, Nell? What is it, my love?" added the old man, leaning towards his wife's wheelchair.

"Ah yes, that's what you said at the time, that he went off with this woman who came. They were in it together. That's what you said, but I wasn't so sure."

Paula ventured a question. "Did they actually go away together?"

"No, they did not," replied Mr. Smith firmly. "He went off in a taxi with his two suitcases. Me and my mate—him that was living next door at that time—we saw him. You were too busy"—and he turned to his wife—"quarrelling with her next door."

They did not remember the man's name; that was perhaps too much to expect. They did not even remember the names of Mr. and Mrs. Martyr. And they had nothing more to tell.

Mr. Smith assured them that he had enjoyed their visit, and that any time they wanted to know any more about Mr. William Mountsey—

"We shall come to you," said Paula, really meaning it.

She shook hands, and then hesitated by the chair of the paralysed old woman, longing to find some way of thanking her.

"Mrs. Smith has enjoyed your visit," said the old man very formally. "It's stirred up her memories, and that does her good."

Back in the narrow pathway between the rhododendron bushes, James lifted Paula off her feet and swung her round in a dance of triumph.

"It's Robin Key."

"It must be."

But almost instantly they sobered up again.

"If he's capable of theft—"

"And all this secrecy—"

"Then what really happened to Eileen?"

Suddenly they were filled with a sense of urgency, although they had no idea what they were going to do.

They returned to the entrance gate and the white-haired woman at the pay desk spoke to them.

"Did you find Mr. and Mrs. Smith?"

"Yes indeed," said James. "They were most helpful."

"And did you like the house?"

"Very much," said Paula. "We hope to come again."

— 13 —

"How far are we from Forest Brook?" asked Paula when the yellow mini was once more on the road.

"About ten miles."

"Wouldn't you think it was too risky for Robin, staying so near to Willing Hall?"

"Yes, you would think so," said James, "but on the other hand he knew the region, which is a great advantage when one is hiding, and it was also important to be within easy reach of Brighton. Presumably Eileen was still there. And if the only people who knew of his connection with Willing Hall were the Smiths and Charles Mountsey—well, I doubt if the Smiths have moved more than ten miles from home base in the last thirty years, and as for Charles—"

"Charles was already too insane to be much of a risk," agreed Paula. "There were the Martyrs, of course, but the Willing Hall period seems to have been something they preferred to forget. They were not happy there. And perhaps Robin Key already owned High Beechwoods. Could he have been the estate agent's clerk as well?"

James thought this quite possible. Robin seemed to be crooked enough to have been anything, and he must also have had something to do with the book trade at some time or other, or he would not have seen the possibilities in Eileen's manuscript.

"Eileen's manuscript. Yes," said Paula. "I'm sure she wrote those early books, but I still feel that it was her mother's voice telling the story. It's not a 1920s or a 1930s voice.

And definitely not a Canadian voice. It's Edwardian England. I believe that Rosie told her dreams, and maybe some of her own experiences, to her daughter, and they caught hold of Eileen's imagination and she made stories out of them.''

For a little while they drove along the green Sussex lanes in silence, thinking about the first Rosie O'Grady, such a very different sort of woman from the second.

She had come to England to find her natural father. But was there also a hope of selling her stories? Railway Cottages knew nothing about her writings. Perhaps she had not intended to publish them until she met Robin Key. Perhaps they contained incidents and characters that William Mountsey would have recognised as founded on fact and preferred not to have made public. In that case, Eileen might have been intending a little blackmail.

But it never came to that because she never met her father, who was already dead, and instead of meeting his eccentric heir, the poet Charles Mountsey, she met Robin Key.

''Who then took over completely,'' said James.

A little later he said, ''Did he marry her?''

''Maybe. I don't think it matters all that much. What matters far more is—''

''Did he murder her?'' said James.

''Yes. We have been thinking it ever since yesterday evening, and now we have said it at last.''

''At any rate, I don't believe in the tuberculosis and the Swiss sanatorium,'' James continued. ''According to Mrs. Martyr, Eileen was very healthy and very tough. And by no means shy and retiring. Why did she agree to all the secrecy after the books were published? You'd have expected her to revel in the publicity.''

It could only be assumed that Robin had a strong hold over her. Perhaps she was involved in the thefts from Willing Hall. And without his help she would never have got into print. But she must have longed to come out into the open as a successful novelist.

''I'm sure that's it,'' said Paula. ''He could keep her quiet for a while by saying it was unsafe to make herself known, and that the mystery business was good for sales, but in the end she would rebel. And he dared not risk having her talk to all and sundry. Probably he had a criminal record even before the Mountsey thefts. So he had to keep her quiet. And there was only one certain way.''

"To kill the goose who was laying the golden eggs," said James. "She would have been a perfect candidate for murder, poor thing. Remote house, no friends or relations. If any of her Canadian connections did start inquiring after her, they'd get no further than Railway Cottages. They would never track her down to High Beechwoods and Robin Key. As far as England was concerned, she was Rosie O'Grady, the romantic novelist, the Mystery Lady whom not even her agent or her publisher had ever met. A perfect victim. A perfect murder. Robin was safe. His only problem was how to produce another novel."

"A very big problem," said Paula, "but George Bruce solved it for him by sending him Joan Cook."

Joan. The thought of her put a stop to their excited speculations. Had she come to the same conclusions as they had themselves?

"If she has," said Paula, "then she won't hesitate to tell him so. She won't mind what risk she takes. She doesn't care what happens to her."

They were travelling now across some open country with grassy picnic places between the clumps of heather. Paula turned the yellow mini into one of these pleasant little parking places.

"James," she said, "I don't think we ought to go to Forest Brook now. I'm just as worried about Joan as you are, but she wanted to handle this herself. We don't know what she has in mind, and we could make things worse by butting in."

James thought they ought to take the risk.

"But supposing they," argued Paula, "that she did come to the conclusion that Robin murdered Eileen and was going to challenge him with it. If he is going to murder Joan he isn't going to wait. He will have done it hours ago. We'd have been too late even if we'd gone straight there from London this morning."

James admitted that this sounded reasonable. "But you can't get rid of people as quickly and easily as all that," he added. "Eileen was different. He'd got plenty of time and she must have been rather stupid. And quite unprepared."

"Exactly," said Paula. "Joan is quite different. I'm sure

she knows exactly what she's doing and she won't thank us for interfering.''

The argument continued for several minutes. Neither of them was aware of the colour of the heather and the surrounding woods, and the distant blue haze beyond which was the sea. A family of teen-age children a few yards away released a model aeroplane. James and Paula watched its course without really seeing it.

"Why don't we find a call-box and telephone Joan," suggested Paula.

"Do it if you want to," said James, "but I'm sure we'll only get the Spanish-housekeeper act."

This seemed only too likely. Eventually Paula gave in, but not with a very good grace.

"We're going to regret this," she said.

They drove to Forest Brook in silence. At the end of the track that led to High Beechwoods, Paula stopped the car.

"Can you see if Robin's mini is there? Or Joan's Renault?"

James got out and walked a little way along the track.

"The mini is there," he said when he returned, "but I can't see any sign of Joan's car."

"Could it be round the other side of the house?"

"I don't think so. There isn't any garage. They park in the drive. Or outside the gate."

"And if I drive in, he won't be able to get out unless I move," said Paula. "You'll have to decide, and decide quickly, whether you really want to have a fight with Robin Key. Maybe he's got a gun. To shoot rabbits, of course."

"You'd better stay here and I'll go alone," said James.

"Don't be silly. If that's what you want, then I'm coming too. He's less likely to act rashly if we block his escape route."

Paula turned the yellow mini into the track. "If he has made away with Joan," she said as they bumped along, "he'll have had to dispose of both the body and the car."

"He could fake a crash," said James. "That's the classic way."

"Where?"

"Disused quarry or something. We don't know the area. He does."

"I don't believe it. Joan's too bright. She won't walk into a trap. And I don't believe in these heroics either."

Paula stopped the yellow mini a few feet behind the red one, got out and slammed the door.

"I wish you'd stay here," said James.

But she was already through the open gate and striding along the path to the front door of High Beechwoods. James caught up with her just as she was ringing the bell."

"I'm almost sure there's nobody here," she said, "but someone's left a message."

A clean white envelope showed up brightly against the cream paint of the door to which it was Sellotaped. Paula pulled it away.

"Dr. Paula Glenning" was typed neatly in the centre.

"We were supposed to find this tomorrow afternoon," she said as she opened the envelope and held the sheet of writing paper for James to read as well.

"Dear Paula," it ran, "I am so sorry that you and James will find nobody here when you come. I enjoyed our talk and am sorry that we cannot meet again, but Robin and I decided that we are both too old and tired now to stand up to the publicity that will inevitably follow the revelations about Rosie O'Grady.

"Even if you keep to your resolution not to publish, you will have no way of restraining George Bruce. No doubt you will show him this letter, and no doubt he will attempt to trace us, but he will not succeed, any more than you will succeed yourself if you decide, after all, to continue with your researches.

"Good-bye, Paula and James. It was nice knowing you."

Under the typescript was a signature: "Rosie O'Grady."

"It's the signature on the contracts," said Paula, "and on all other documents concerning the novels. It could have been written by either of them."

"The letter could too." James pressed the bell again. "Robin could have written it to put us off the scent while all the time Joan's lying there dead of an overdose."

"It wouldn't be like that," insisted Paula. "If it were a faked suicide, we'd find Joan dead in the car with a pipe from the exhaust. And a typed confession. I'm sure she's not dead, either here or anywhere else. And I'm sure she wrote this letter. It sounds like her. It's both tough and good-tempered. And it's laughing at us. Just like when we were here. It's got her tone of voice and that's something very difficult to copy.''

"But if Joan wrote this letter of her own free will," said James slowly, "then she never intended us to meet again, and all this business of challenging Robin—"

"Exactly," said Paula. "I think she is very clever indeed and we are very stupid. But in fairness to us, I don't think we'd have been so easily misled if we hadn't been feeling so guilty about our house-breaking."

"Paula," said James, leaning against the door, "my mind is reeling. You don't mean that Joan's whole story was made up, and that she is in it too?"

"I'm quite sure she is 'in it,' whatever that may mean, and she admitted herself that she's a good actress. But actually I think a lot of the story was true, which made it all the more convincing."

"I certainly believed the part about her childhood and her marriage and her working for George and being sent here," said James.

"So did I. And I still believe it. It's the part about Robin Key that we found difficult to swallow, about her not having had any suspicions of him. We were both uneasy about it, weren't we? But we've been so taken up with our own discoveries about Eileen and so sure that Robin murdered her—"

"Are you suggesting that it was Joan who killed her?" broke in James.

"I hope not. I like to think not, but I'm sure she knew about it. Or guessed. And I would guess that when we saw Robin yesterday morning, he was intending to go to Joan's home and arrange with her to wind up Rosie O'Grady and for them both to disappear, but we followed him and he couldn't shake us off and had to change the plan. And when he got clear of us at last, he would surely telephone her, and maybe they arranged together that she should come here and check that they hadn't left any clues and then clear out. But she found us here and so the plan had to be changed yet again."

James thought this over. "She saw the opportunity to find out how much we knew," he said at last, "and took it."

"Yes. As I said, we felt guilty. And we were quite definitely in the wrong. But she must have been laughing at us from the very first. That phone call made to Robin was meant to divert our suspicions, and maybe to give him a signal at the same time. She must have called him again as soon as we had gone. He probably came here at once and they checked through the house to make sure there was nothing that would help anybody to trace them, and then went off in Joan's car."

"I've got the number of Joan's car," said James.

"That's better than nothing, but I think we'll find it parked at an airport. Or in the docks at Dover."

"So what do we do now?" asked James.

"I suppose it really depends," said Paula slowly, "on whether we feel quite sure that there was a murder committed. I mean," she went on, trying to sort out her own confused thoughts, "that if I was convinced that no serious crime was involved, then I could tell George Bruce that I hadn't been able to get in touch with anybody at this address and that I hadn't been able to find out anything worth writing about. He'd have to accept that, I think, and I should be free of it all."

"But it wouldn't be true, and you're no good at lying."

"I know," agreed Paula.

"And personally I do think there's been a crime committed. I'm becoming more and more sure that somebody killed Eileen. Aren't you?"

"Yes," said Paula even more unhappily than before. "I wish I weren't."

"So what do we do now?"

"Tell George everything, I suppose. I'll write out a report this evening and try to get an appointment with him tomorrow. Then it's up to him to decide."

Paula opened up the typewritten letter and read it again.

"I liked her so much," she said sadly, "but I'm sure she was lying. Let's get away from this place. It's horrible. Even the cat's deserted it. Come on."

James walked back to the yellow mini with her, held open the door of the driver's seat, and then said, "Just a minute. I want to look at something. Won't be long." And he returned to the house, leaving Paula brooding over the letter.

Perhaps after all it had been written by Robin. Perhaps,

after all, Joan was completely innocent of deception and was actually in danger. But she was not completely innocent of deception, Paula reminded herself, because she had dressed up and visited the agent and the publisher and pretended to be Rosie O'Grady. A real Rosie O'Grady.

That must have taken not only very good acting but also a lot of nerve. Joan Cook plainly had both. But what a strange character she was. What was her motive in taking on the job of Mystery Lady, thus condemning herself to a kind of living death?

Those had been her very words. Even at the time Paula had felt them to be rather too melodramatic, but such was the force of Joan's personality that she had accepted them, together with everything else that Joan had said. The impression she had given, of a strong and intelligent woman full of sad regret, had been overwhelming. Perhaps there had been some truth behind the acting.

The motive, then. Money, of course. Joan liked what money could buy. The pretty cottage in the pretty village would, Paula suspected, be full of beautiful things. Perhaps there was another pretty dwelling in some other part of the world.

Money, and perhaps power. Secret power, not the primitive craving for recognition and admiration that had probably brought Eileen to her death. The second Rosie O'Grady was a much more subtle character.

Was she also a ruthless one? Had they got the whole thing the wrong way round, so that it was not Joan who was in danger from Robin Key, but Robin who was in danger from Joan? He was very shrewd, but if it came to a battle of wits, Joan would be the winner. She had actually written the books, and he had been the essential link with the outside world.

Therefore, as Joan had said herself, they needed each other, but she had said it in a way that aroused pity: the lonely widow needing to be needed. It could be looked at in quite a different way: the poor working girl seeing the chance of making a fortune. Nothing wrong with that, except that it was not the character that she had projected.

And as for their mutual dependence, what would happen if there were to be no more books? As Rosie O'Grady, Joan was written out. She had said so herself, and George Bruce had complained that the last few novels were not up to standard. Presumably there was still plenty of money somewhere, but it could well be that each one of them, Robin and Joan, would feel safer if the other one was out of the way.

At this point in her reflections Paula decided that it was pointless to think about it any longer. She stuffed the typewritten letter into her shoulder-bag, looked up to see that the sky was clouding over again, and glanced at her watch.

Half past five. Where on earth was James? What they needed now was to get away from this God-forsaken place and find somewhere that served tea. Somewhere commonplace and comforting that belonged to the ordinary everyday world.

Where was James? Was he trying to break into the house again? Had he succeeded?

Suddenly Paula was struck with a notion that made her jump out of the yellow mini and run towards the house. Why had they both been so sure that the house was empty? The bell had not been answered, but that meant nothing. The letter had been intended to drive them away. Or had it? Had it been intended to arouse their curiosity? After all, they had broken in once: why not again?

Were Robin and Joan, or one or the other of them, waiting silently inside all this time to see whether the bait had worked? In other words, had she and James walked into a trap?

—— *14* ——

She rang the bell and banged on the door; ran on to the long windows of the sitting-room, found that the curtains were drawn across and she could not see in, and ran round to the back door and banged on that.

It opened so suddenly that she tripped and nearly fell.

"James—oh James! Thank God you're all right."

He shut the door behind her and Paula turned and noticed the damage.

"The bolt wasn't very strong. I really did break in this time," he said.

Paula looked more closely at the splintered wood, but she was so relieved to see him alive and well that she couldn't find any words of reproach.

"And there's nobody here?"

"No one. Come and see."

She looked first round the kitchen. The fridge was empty and the door left ajar. There were some cans of food in a cupboard, and jars of tea and coffee and other dry goods. The old-fashioned gas water-heater over the sink had been switched off, likewise all electric appliances in the utility room and in the bathroom.

The living-room was dim, with the heavy curtains drawn across. Paula turned the light switch, but no light came.

"Turned off at the mains," said James.

He pulled the curtains aside to let in a little daylight. The faded roses had gone, but otherwise there seemed to be no change in the room, except that it looked more desolate than ever.

"They've disconnected the telephone as well," he said. "So there'd have been no point in calling. And the desk drawers are unlocked and empty. I wish I'd had a chance to look in them yesterday."

"Probably nothing really important there." Paula walked over to the bookshelves. "The early novels are still here." She pulled out one of the first hardback editions and looked at the inside cover. "Yes, that's the handwriting. The same as in the first letter to the literary agent. That's the Rosie O'Grady signature, except that it's Eileen's. Our only clue, and we've exhausted it. I suppose they knew it didn't matter and that's why they left the books here. Did you look in the bedrooms?"

"Only in one of them. That's when I heard you at the back door. I didn't come to the front because I was using the bathroom. The water's turned off too, by the way."

"I suppose we'd better look in the other rooms," said Paula, following James into the blue bedroom. The raincoat and the rubber boots had been removed. Apart from the bedcover, there was nothing on the bed.

James opened the door of the yellow room, the bedroom that Joan had used. "I've been round everywhere else," he said.

The books and the flower vase on the bedside table were gone. Paula knew before she opened the cupboards that there would be nothing there. And the lemon-yellow bedspread was stretched flat over the divan bed.

James looked at Paula with sympathy. "It looks as if you're right. They've cleared out together."

"Yes." Paula touched the table where she had found the treasured old copy of *Jane Eyre*. "There's no point staying here. I'll write up that report for George Bruce as soon as I can. Let's go home, James. I hate this house. Joan gave it life and character, but if she too—"

Paula did not finish the sentence. It was at that moment that they heard so surprising a sound in this dead and empty house that for a few seconds they did not realize what it was.

Then Paula knelt down beside the bed and lifted the yellow cover. The sound came again: a plaintive mewing.

It took more than a few seconds to tempt the black cat out from her hiding place under the bed. At last she came, and Paula picked her up and stroked her and looked at James.

"Did you find any of the windows open?" she asked.

"They were all tight shut. And all the doors too."

"Then this might make a lot of difference. Joan really loved this cat. She would never have left her shut up in an abandoned house. And the cat's frightened, James. She ran away from Robin when we first came here. She wouldn't have hidden away from Joan."

James agreed. The last one to leave the house must have been Robin, not Joan. And they could not have left together, because Joan would have made sure that the cat was not locked in. So that, perhaps, after all—

The cat seemed to want to go to James. Paula let her go and she sprang onto his shoulder and wrapped herself round his neck.

"I'm going to leave that little window open," said Paula, "so that she can come in for shelter if she wants to and get out when she wants."

"There's no need," said James. "I'm going to take her home. I am adopting this animal, and there are no prizes for guessing what I am going to call her."

After a moment of surprise Paula reached up and fondled the cat's ears. "Hello, Rosie," she said. "Rosie O'Grady the Third. Or is it the Fourth?"

When they were seated in the yellow mini, Rosie descended from James's shoulders to his knees and went to sleep. Paula switched on the engine, but still hesitated to shift the car.

"Problem?" said James. "I'll reverse back to the road, if you like, and save you a pain in the neck."

"It's not that. I can manage. It's just that I wish we could find some clue."

"We have found a clue." James stroked the cat, who produced a purr.

"Yes, oh yes indeed. This makes it much more likely that Joan is innocent. But it also makes it more likely that she is in danger."

"Do you want to go searching for her body?" asked James.

"I suppose it's silly. But we shan't come here again."

"All right."

Rosie O'Grady the Third or Fourth, still half-asleep, was placed on the back seat of the yellow mini with the doors firmly closed.

"There's nothing in Robin's car," said James after a close examination of the red mini. "In any case it's probably only a second car and not registered in that name. He'll have a Mercedes somewhere."

"If only we could find where."

They walked round the garden. There was an old shed that was unlocked and contained a few geraniums in pots, a lawn mower, and a small selection of essential gardening tools.

"I suppose they took it in turns to keep the garden looking presentable," said Paula, "but they can't have troubled very much in recent years. There's little attempt to make the place look like the hideout of a reclusive lady novelist. They could have made a much more convincing setting if they'd wanted to."

"And Joan could have acted the part if necessary."

"Innocent or guilty, she was tired of it," said Paula, looking up at the slope of beech trees. "I suppose there's no point exploring the woods?"

James was examining the privet hedge. There was no gate, no way out from the garden into the woods, and no sign of anyone having made a gap in the hedge.

"If there's a body buried there," he said, "it's a job for the police. And if it's been there for more than thirty years—"

Paula turned away. "The farm? They must know something. Or at any rate suspect something. We could always make the excuse that we'd like to have the cat."

"Farm cats fend for themselves," said James. "They won't worry when she doesn't come back."

From the front gate of High Beechwoods they could see over the hedge down the hill. Several fields away were the red-tiled roofs of the farmhouse and its outbuildings. There was no sign of life in the fields. It was very obvious that James did not want to call there. Neither did Paula, but still she could not tear herself away.

"Even if nobody else ever came here at all," she said, "the mail van must have come. How did they deliver parcels? Copies of books, and so on?"

"I would guess that they arranged to collect all mail from the main post office in Tonbridge or Maidstone," said James wearily. "They'll have thought of everything."

"Joan's pretty village. Surely it can't be very far from Maidstone?"

"There's dozens of pretty villages not very far from Maidstone," said James with enthusiasm. "It's quite a big town."

"I suppose we'd better go home, then."

"I don't know about you," said James, "but I'm getting awfully hungry. And I'm sure Rosie O'Grady the Fourth is hungry too."

They left High Beechwoods without even a farewell glance. Paula was craning her head round for the long backward drive down the track, and James was very occupied with the cat.

The drive back to London seemed interminable. Apart from a few comments on the traffic or on the state of the roads, they did not speak. In James's ground-floor apartment at the edge of Hampstead Heath, Paula lay back in an armchair and closed her eyes while he made tea for them both and brought milk for the cat.

"I've had enough driving practice to last the rest of the year," she said. After she had rested for a while, she got up and said she was going home to write up her report while it was still fresh in her mind, even if it meant sitting up half the night, and that she would bring it to James for comment before getting in touch with George.

She left him fussing over Rosie O'Grady the Fourth, wondering whether it was safe to let her out into the garden or whether he had better make a dirt tray, and debating the relative merits of a can of sardines or some cold roast chicken that was in the fridge.

Paula advised the chicken and to keep Rosie indoors for a few days until she was used to her new home.

"Whatever else may come of the Mystery Lady," she said, laughing at him, "there's one thing for sure: a very pampered cat."

— 15 —

When Paula got home, still very tired from her long day's driving, she found that her attic haven did not bring the usual degree of consolation. For the first time since she had moved in, twelve years previously, after the breakup of her marriage, she had the sense of something lacking, and for a little while she almost wished that she had thought of giving a home to the last of the Rosies herself.

The empty feeling did not last long. As soon as she sat down to work on the report for George Bruce, the apartment felt as if it contained life again.

"What did George Bruce want me to do?" she wrote at the head of a sheet of lined foolscap paper, as if copying out an examination question the better to fix it in her mind.

The answer came at once: to investigate the life and work of the person who writes under the name of Rosie O'Grady and to write a popular book about her that would appeal both to the many readers of the novels and also to people who had some pretensions to literary scholarship.

Then she asked herself, What was my method of research? and gave herself the reply that it had been slapdash and un-methodical; and to the question What have I discovered? she replied that there was no single person who wrote under the pen-name of Rosie O'Grady, but that three women and one man were between them responsible for the novels. On which one of these should she concentrate?

"The first woman," wrote Paula, "was actually called by that name. She was a milliner's apprentice, living in humble

112

circumstances in Brighton. The source of my information is a very old lady who was a neighbour of the family. Her evidence is reliable but incomplete. She can tell of the childhood and adolescence of Rosie but little more, but she insists that Rosie O'Grady was barely literate and would certainly not have been able to write the sort of manuscript that was sent to the literary agent.

"It is not impossible that in later years, when my witness had lost touch with Rosie, the latter taught herself to write more efficiently. My witness says that Rosie had dreams of grandeur. If she had been able to write them down, they might well have come out in some such form as the early novels, and I think it very likely that she was the inspiration for those books, though not the actual author."

Paula thought for a moment or two, and then wrote a summary of what Mrs. Martyr had said about Rosie O'Grady. It was possible, she continued, that Mrs. Martyr might remember a little more, but there would remain an enormous gap. The only other possible source of information about Rosie was Robin Key, who could not possibly have met her, but might have heard about her from another source. He would be dealt with more fully under the next two entries.

The second woman was Eileen O'Grady, illegitimate daughter of Rosie. Sources of information: Mrs. Martyr, as above. Largely hearsay evidence, but probably fairly reliable. Mr. and Mrs. Smith of the Willing Hall estate in Sussex. Marginal evidence, but if reliable, very important. Third, and most important of all, the evidence of Joan Cook (the third of the three women, to be dealt with later).

Paula quickly wrote down what Mrs. Martyr had said about Eileen, and added that Mrs. Smith remembered a woman, who was probably Eileen, coming to Willing Hall. She then paused to think hard before writing down what Joan Cook had said about Eileen O'Grady, whom Joan had not called "Eileen," but whom she had referred to as "Rosie" or "Rosamund," wife of Robin Key.

Again she stopped to think, and eventually continued: "How far can one rely on the evidence of Joan Cook? I believe that the Eileen whom Mrs. Martyr described, and the Rosie or Rosamund whom Joan Cook spoke of, were one and the same woman, and that this woman was the author of the first four novels and probably of the first draft of the fifth. But I think that everything else that Joan Cook told us about this woman is untrue. The impression she gave of a timid, dependent creature already suffering from the consumption that was finally to kill her is in great contrast to Mrs. Martyr's picture of a tough, healthy, self-assertive and ambitious woman. I believe Mrs. Martyr's version to be the correct one.

"The inscription in the books, 'All my love and thanks' (not mentioned by Joan but discovered without her knowledge) might perhaps point to the clinging character, but it could equally well have been written by the tough, ambitious character in sincere gratitude and affection to the man who had helped her so much.

"Eileen, according to Joan, wished to hide herself away from the world instead of claiming her fame.

"Eileen, according to Mrs. Martyr, would be the sort who would want to publicize herself. On the other hand, Eileen, according to Mrs. Martyr, could be very secretive if she chose, and according to the evidence of Mr. and Mrs. Smith, there were good practical reasons why she and Robin Key should not seek publicity.

"It seems a reasonable supposition," Paula went on, "that as the Rosie O'Grady novels became more and more successful, Eileen began to chafe more and more at the need for secrecy, and it is reasonable to assume that this caused friction between herself and Robin Key."

At this point in her writing Paula got up to make coffee. When she returned to her desk, she wrote:

"The evidence concerning Rosie O'Grady is too scanty to make a book. The evidence concerning her daughter Eileen is so conflicting that it cannot form the basis for a biography. Such a life would require the full co-operation of Robin Key, and this is hardly likely to be forthcoming."

On to the third woman, Joan Cook.

Paula wrote a summary of the conversation with Joan, adding a few remarks about the house itself, but omitting the fact that James had been with her, and that they had broken in.

"How much is Joan Cook's evidence to be relied on?" she concluded. "Did she present this false view of Eileen knowing it to be false? Or did she genuinely believe everything that Robin had told her about Eileen, and pass it on in all sincerity?

"Joan Cook is to me much the most interesting of the three women concerned in the novels of Rosie O'Grady. Perhaps because I have met her. Perhaps because she seems to be a much more complex character than either of the other two. Her life could make a most interesting book, but the main source of material would have to be Joan herself, and she would not consent to anybody else writing the book. She said so herself."

Now came the one man, Robin Key, the link between both "Rosie O'Gradys" and the outside world. He had been in contact with more people concerned in the publication of the novels than had either of the two women. Joan Cook was, in fact, known to George Bruce, though not under that name, but Robin Key was known to George Bruce in his own name and in his own character. The publisher would no doubt have formed his own impressions, and all Paula could do was to state hers.

Robin Key had not wanted to talk to her at all, and being obliged to do so, had first tried to put her off the scent and then to run away. He appeared to be very self-confident and not in the least bit nervous, but nevertheless he must have something to fear. From Joan Cook's story (if true), it appeared that he was trying to conceal the fact that there had been two Rosie O'Gradys.

But why should it matter to him so much if this came to light?

The answer could lie in Mr. and Mrs. Smith's evidence. If he was indeed the same man as the one who had once worked for Charles Mountsey (and Paula here added that she was convinced that he was), then he was certainly a liar, very likely a thief, and probably guilty of other crimes as well. "I do not believe that Eileen died in a Swiss sanatorium," wrote Paula. "I believe that she posed a threat to Robin and that he decided she had to be got rid of."

She added a few more sentences and then wrote "This is the end of the summing up of my researches. Three women and one man. What is now my own position? I have contracted to write the life of Rosie O'Grady, but it is surely obvious from the foregoing that there is no way in which I can satisfactorily carry out this task.

"What does George Bruce want me to do? What did he want me to do when he commissioned me to undertake this inquiry? Ought I perhaps to have said, Not three women and one man, but three women and *two* men?"

Paula glanced at her watch. It was long past midnight. She got up and made more coffee, spread a slice of bread and butter and ate it absentmindedly, and then returned to her desk and continued to write, covering the sheets of the lined foolscap paper with her neat small handwriting.

"The evidence of George Bruce. It is like the evidence of the dog that barked in the night in the Sherlock Holmes story. The dog did not bark. That was the evidence. George Bruce gave me practically no information at all. That was his evidence.

"Why? Because he wanted me to approach my subject with an open mind. Fair enough.

"But was it fair to withhold completely the absolutely vital information that he had actually sent a member of his own editorial staff to find out who was writing the Rosie O'Grady books, and what part Robin Key played in them?

"No, it was not fair. I was given the impression that he had employed a private detective, not that his own business was involved. That much of Joan's story, about his sending her on this mission, I do believe.

"And was it fair of George Bruce to write a letter of introduction to Robin Key that specifically stated that I was interested only in the novels, not in a biography? No, it was not fair.

"I do not believe that I was employed to write the life of Rosie O'Grady at all. I was employed to investigate a mystery, and it was put to me in the way that would tempt me most.

"Why should George Bruce want the Mystery Lady investigated when he already knew so much about her himself?

"George Bruce has had plenty of contact with Robin Key. He must know far more about Robin than I am ever going to be able to discover.

"He knows about Joan and her abilities. He knows there has been more than one Rosie O'Grady. He must have suspected, after Joan's disappearance, that she was in fact writing the books. He knows about the change of style.

"He must have known, or suspected, that it was Joan who came to the office that day in the guise of Rosie O'Grady.

"He has been willing to go along all these years with the deception, conspiracy, whatever one likes to call it, that lies behind the cult of the Mystery Lady. It has been a very profitable business, but it could not go on for ever.

"Then why did George not get together with Robin and Joan and the three of them decide how to kill off Rosie O'Grady?''

Paula stopped to think for a moment.

"Perhaps, after all, that was not so simple. Disposing of a real body is difficult, but disposing of a mythical person can also present problems. Rosie O'Grady would have merited television and radio news items, obituaries in the newspapers. And somewhere there would have had to be a body for some sort of funeral ceremony. And even if that was all successfully accomplished, it would not be the end of it. The Mystery Lady would be dead but she would refuse to lie down. Interest in her would remain, people wanting to write articles on her, scholars researching . . .

"Suppose they discussed all this and decided that both the myth and the mystery had to be exploded. But not by one of themselves. It would make a better impression to bring in somebody from outside who knew nothing about the situation at all, but who had recently done some quite successful literary investigation. Let her find out what she could and write about it. If it made a good story, let it be published, suitably edited, of course, so that George Bruce came across as a victim of deception and not its instigator.

"Joan and Robin would presumably get their share of the profits and be willing to disappear. Neither had a public position to keep up, and they were both getting sick of Rosie O'Grady. In any case the published story would not use real names or places.

"Mrs. Martyr? Caroline?

"Ah, a very different matter here. Two very real people who would not consent to be spirited away.

"And neither had Eileen consented to be spirited away. But Eileen could not have been in the conspiracy too because she was dead.

"Up till Eileen's death there had been no conspiracy—at least, not one in which George was involved.

"Unless he joined forces with the other two in murdering

Eileen because she could no longer write the money-spinning books. In which case Joan was in it from the very beginning, and Robin, even if he struck the fatal blow or administered the fatal dose, was no more guilty than the other two.''

Paula paused for a while on this theory. It fitted the facts and dispensed with the unlikelihood that George himself had been so unsuspecting for all these years. But unfortunately the theory contained one great improbability that out-weighed all its attractions.

George Bruce was a very devious character indeed, who apparently not only believed in, but also acted on, the theory that there was no difference between truth and fiction. He would go to great lengths to obtain startling and original books to publish. But not even he would go so far as to set in train an investigation that could lead to unveiling the fact that he was accessory to a murder.

''And Eileen was murdered,'' wrote Paula at the bottom of the sheet of paper she had just completed. ''I am quite sure of that.''

On that certainty she went to bed at last.

''But you can't give this to George Bruce to read,'' said James the next morning after he had read Paula's draft.

''Why not? Hallo, Rosie,'' she added as the black cat, already quite at home, came from James's kitchen into the sitting-room and sniffed at her ankles.

''You can't tell him you think he's been involved in a conspiracy, let alone accuse him of being an accessory to murder,'' said James.

''I've written a truthful account of the investigation. I believe in getting at the truth even if he doesn't. Don't you, James?''

''Well yes, I suppose I do. But this isn't tactful. In fact, it might even be rather unwise, to say the least.''

''I'm not at all afraid that he could try to murder me,'' said Paula cheerfully, ''if that's what you are thinking. But I've got to get out of this business somehow. In my covering letter I've said that I cannot possibly write the book and that I will refund the advance, less the expenses that I've incurred. And once that is agreed, I'm going to forget about all the Rosies except this nice black furry one here.''

"It's not like you to give up," said James after they had argued for a little longer.

"I never wanted to do the job in the first place, and I feel as if I'm being used."

"All the more reason to go on and expose them."

Paula said nothing. Rosie O'Grady the Fourth was now investigating her shoulder-bag, which lay beside her on the settee.

"Or is this just because you want to get rid of me and go on with your researches alone?" said James.

Paula denied this vigorously. Of course not. She had made her decision after the talk with Joan Cook. Without James's help she would have got nowhere. It had been lovely running around detecting with him and she couldn't thank him enough.

Her protestations met with no response. Rosie O'Grady had moved over to James's chair and he was trying to disentangle her claws from the upholstery. When he had succeeded he said, "Then have you any objection to my hunting around by myself? I don't suppose for a moment that I shall uncover anything more, but if I do, I'll let you know."

Paula had not objection. "You'll see I've said nothing about you in my report to George Bruce," she said. "I thought you'd prefer me not to. If he is really in league with Joan and Robin, then presumably they will have told him about you being with me, and it's up to you to explain if you get into difficulties."

"Of course it's up to me. I've no right to be in this at all. That's understood. What I can't understand is your own attitude. How can you not want to know what has happened to Joan?"

"I do want to know, very much indeed," said Paula. "I'm so afraid that our first theory is right after all and that she told Robin she believed he had killed Eileen and that he . . . But I just don't know what to do next. I can't see anything but a blank wall. Maybe after I've talked to George Bruce . . . But if you can see any possible way out yourself, then it's better you go hunt for it on your own."

"I see," said James slowly, allowing Rosie O'Grady to pretend to bite his finger. "Yes. I see."

Paula stood up. "I'd like to get this report to George to-day."

James got up too. "May I have a copy? It could be useful."

"Of course. And I'll let you know what his reactions are. That could be useful too."

"Thanks."

The front door of the apartment closed behind Paula. James returned to the living-room and sat down on the settee beside Rosie O'Grady, who was now vigorously licking her hind legs.

"It's not the right moment," he said, addressing the cat. "It's never going to be the right moment. There'll always be some excuse or another. She's afraid of committing herself, Rosie. I know, because I used to be like that myself. But it's different as one gets older."

Rosie O'Grady did a little somersault and started to wash behind the ears.

"We're both of us getting older," went on James, "Paula and I. We wouldn't want any children and we're not wildly in love. But we know each other. Very well indeed. And we like each other. Very much indeed. And she seems to have learned to accept some help sometimes instead of always being so fiercely independent."

Rosie O'Grady, after several false attempts, managed to anchor her tail under one of her front paws and to hold it still for washing.

James got up and searched for his address book, eventually finding it on the kitchen table. His cleaning woman was on holiday; the apartment was not so tidy as it normally was, and he wondered what Mrs. Lumley would say when she got back to find Rosie in possession.

"So what does Paula really want?" he asked the cat as he sat down again and picked up the extension telephone. "Is she afraid that I'm going to let her down? I won't, you know, Rosie. I think we'd suit each other and be happy. Oh well. Maybe one day it will be the right moment. Meanwhile . . ."

There was no reply from Caroline Martyr's number. He made a note of it and decided to call again in half an hour's time.

16

"I thought we'd better meet here in the office," said George Bruce, "because although people in restaurants are usually talking too much themselves to overhear anybody else, one can never be quite sure. I don't think this room has ever been bugged."

He felt under the desk, pushed aside a corner of the carpet with his foot and kicked it back, pulled out a couple of books from a shelf and peered into the gap before replacing them.

It was a high, book-lined room on the first floor of an early-nineteenth-century house in a short cul-de-sac five minutes' walk from Piccadilly Circus. The general impression was weighty and sombre—dark mahogany, dark Persian carpet—with George himself providing the colour and the life.

Paula, made more apprehensive than ever by his clowning, sat in one of the two dark-red leather armchairs by the long window, and at last he joined her there.

"I think we are safe," he said in the low tones of a conspirator in a melodrama. "Let us commence our deliberations."

"There's really nothing I need to say," said Paula. "I've written it all down. I'd like to know whether you agree to my expenses, that's all, before I write the cheque."

Nervousness and irritation made her sound very abrupt. George offered cigarettes and she accepted one against her will.

"Now, let's see." He reached behind him and picked up a sheet of paper from the desk. "Travelling expenses. This seems to be very modest."

"I've only got a mini," said Paula. "It doesn't use much petrol."

Thank goodness I did buy my own car, she was thinking; it might just be possible to keep James out of this.

"Willing Hall," said George, continuing to read from the piece of paper. "Charles Mountsey's place. What's it like?"

"I never actually saw the house," replied Paula. "I was too busy talking to the old couple in the cottage."

"They knew old Charles, did they?"

"Yes. Very well. They were the only people who saw him at all during the last years."

"Extraordinary. He must have been quite mad. But that's when the best of the poems were written. Do you know those later ones?"

"I didn't before. I read them for the first time a few days ago."

"That very short one—'The Inner Night.' I've got it here somewhere. In an anthology."

George got up and found the book and continued to talk about Charles Mountsey's poetry.

I have been here for over fifteen minutes, said Paula to herself, and we have not once mentioned Rosie O'Grady. Are we not to talk about her at all? Is that the plan?

It seemed that it was.

"There's not much written about Mountsey," mused George. "He's hardly a major poet, but he deserves at least one good study. And it's an old family. No shortage of material. I think this could well be the answer to our problem. It's much more in your line. Academic stuff. No reason why it shouldn't be quite popular—though, of course, it hasn't got the feminist appeal of *Shadowed Lives*. How about it, Paula? Wouldn't you like to do a really good job on Charles Mountsey, his life and works? It would give me great pleasure to publish it."

Paula had the sensation of being dragged back from the point of escape and replaced firmly in the trap. The trouble was that the suggestion really did interest her. A minor twentieth-century poet was much more in her line than Rosie O'Grady. If only this suggestion had been made to her first. But no. She must get clear of George Bruce. Now and for ever.

"I can't take on any Mountsey research," she said rather less firmly than she had intended. "I need a holiday."

"Of course, of course. It's a holiday season. I'm going away myself next week. We'll talk about it later in more detail. But there will be no need for a fresh contract. We can alter and initial the relevant clause on the other one. And there's no need for any financial transactions. These expenses can quite easily apply to the Mountsey book."

Paula stood up. It was pointless to keep reiterating that she was not going to write it, and it was equally pointless to say any more about the money. She would pay the advance back somehow. Perhaps James would be able to give some advice.

And then she remembered that she was trying not to slip into this habit of consulting James over everything, and her moment of hesitation was instantly recognized and seized on by George Bruce.

"Go and have a good holiday. You've earned it. And we'll deal with Mountsey when you get back."

They were both at the door of the room before Paula was able to say, "But what about Rosie O'Grady?"

"You've produced a fascinating piece of fiction, my dear, but unfortunately I don't think we are going to be able to use it."

"Why not?"

"Because people are so credulous. They will persist in believing things that are obviously invention."

"So you do believe, after all, that there is such a thing as truth?"

They were standing several feet apart, and Paula looked straight at him as she spoke, and for the first time in their acquaintance she had the impression that he was not quite in command of himself.

"Did I ever say I didn't?" he said after a short pause.

"No," she admitted, "not exactly. But you said it didn't matter. That it was fiction and myth that governed human life."

"Quite correct."

Paula had expected him to continue, but when he did not do so she spoke herself. "There is some truth, then, in my record? Aren't you afraid I might make it public—magazine articles, radio broadcasts?"

"Go ahead. Do so. It's you, in the end, who will look very foolish when Rosie O'Grady appears in person on television to give the lie to all you've said. The viewers, the readers, the audience are all conditioned to believe in an old-lady novelist of that name. They aren't conditioned to believe in this mass of contradictory speculation that you have produced, my dear Paula.''

"So you're not afraid?''

"I'm not afraid. I'm very grateful to you. Your researches have filled in a very vital gap. I suspected something and now I know for sure. I hoped you might find out and you have. Well done, Paula.''

"You mean that Robin Key murdered Eileen O'Grady?''

"I'm not saying what I mean. But I'm grateful to you.''

He made a move towards the door, but Paula remained where she stood. "If you are so sure of being able to produce an old-lady novelist,'' she said, "does that mean that you know Joan Cook is alive and well?''

George had opened the door, but he shut it again and replied in a voice so resentful that she was convinced he was sincere: "Why shouldn't Joan be well? God knows she's had enough money out of the business.''

"I'm sure she has,'' murmured Paula, playing for time because she had the feeling that she might be breaking through at last, that George's bitterness against Joan was fighting with his caution.

For a moment or two the outcome hung in the balance. Then he said abruptly, "Come and sit down again. I'd like your opinion on something.''

There was a knock at the door. "I'm not to be disturbed,'' said George to the secretary who stood there. "Nobody at all. Not till I say so.''

The door closed again and Paula resumed her seat.

"What makes you think there might be anything the matter with Joan?'' asked George.

"I didn't put it in my report,'' said Paula, "but in fact on our—I mean on my second visit to High Beechwoods, Joan had disappeared. Gone away. Leaving a note stuck to the door. We—I mean I—''

"Cut out the 'I' and 'we' stuff,'' snapped George. "I never supposed for a moment that you were working on this alone. Who've you been running around with? Richard Grieve?''

"No. James Goff.''

"The fact that I didn't want anybody else to know about your investigations didn't matter, I suppose?''

"If it hadn't been for his help, I'd have learned nothing at all," said Paula with spirit.

"Okay. I'll grant you that." There was a hint of a return to his usual genial manner before he began to look black again. "They've been very clever and exceptionally lucky. I never got very far in my own inquiries, and I did try to find out what happened to Joan."

"Yes, she said so," said Paula, but forbore to add that George could not have tried very hard to track Joan down nor to find out who was actually writing the books. It must have suited him well to have a steady supply of O'Grady novels without ever having the nuisance of being deferential to their author. It was only when the supply looked like coming to an end that he began seriously to interest himself in the identity of the Mystery Lady.

"If I'd guessed, when I sent her to chase up Robin Key, that she'd go and rat on me like that . . ." went on George.

There was no doubt at all that Paula's uncovering of Joan had been a revelation to him, and it was the money side of it that was annoying him most. If Joan had remained in his employment as an editor, then she would have simply been paid her salary, even if it involved practically rewriting every O'Grady manuscript that came into the office. But as Rosie O'Grady herself, the earnings were in a different category altogether, and it was this that George could not endure.

Paula kept quiet and tried to maintain an expression of sympathetic interest, although in fact she could not feel much sympathy. He had, in a sense, been the victim of a deception, and that, for such an egoist, would be painful; but on the other hand he had himself done very well indeed out of the O'Grady books. Joan had written the great majority of them; why should she not get her full reward?

Eventually he appeared to realize that he was not making a very good impression, and seemed to make some effort to behave in a more appropriate manner.

"You do see, don't you, Paula, that it really is impossible to publish anything along the lines of this draft that you have given me?"

Paula agreed eagerly. Of course she realized that. She had, in fact, tried to make it plain that she could not carry out the assignment, and she was most grateful for the suggestion that she should work on Charles Mountsey instead.

She had not meant to say this; it slipped out before she could stop it. George was himself again, and was having his usual hypnotic effect upon her.

"On the other hand," he went on, ignoring her remarks, "it does make a good story. Mystery Lady exposed. It's a much better story than the Christie disappearance, but it's got to be handled right. We'll have to talk about it. You and James Goff and myself. The scholar sleuths. Yes, I like that. If it were presented in the right way—what d'you think, Paula?"

"I'm sure you're right," murmured Paula, beginning to wonder whether George Bruce was himself not quite sane, so rapidly did he switch from one point of view to another, and so certain did he seem to be that he could get everybody to do exactly what he wanted.

"But perhaps the best person to write it would be Joan," he said. "No offence to you, Paula, but you see: Your book would be an investigation and hers would be a confession, and confessions are the bigger draw. Rosie Confesses. You see what I mean?"

"Yes," said Paula, wondering how ever she was going to bring him down to earth. He seemed to have forgotten that Joan had disappeared again, possibly for ever.

He was walking around now, filling the whole room with his vision of this superstory. Perhaps he was always like this; perhaps this was the secret of his success, a complete ignoring of inconvenient realities. Paula longed for an interruption, but there was not going to be one. He had given instructions to that effect.

Rescue came in the form of yet another of those sudden disconcerting changes of mood. He sat down again, produced more cigarettes, and spoke quite calmly. "But of course we'll have to get hold of Joan. Where did you say she was?"

Paula explained again about finding the house empty, and produced Joan's letter.

George read it without comment. "What did you do next?"

"Broke into the house and looked everywhere to see if we could find some clue as to what had happened. But there was nothing. Only the cat."

"If she went off in a hurry she wouldn't know the cat was in the house," said George after Paula had explained.

"That's right," she agreed, enormously relieved to find that he was capable of rational discussion and praying that this mood would last. "But it would have to be in a very great hurry indeed. Or not of her own free will. She really loved cats."

"I see." He sat thinking for a moment.

"The police?" suggested Paula tentatively. "We've got the number of Joan's car."

He nodded and said, "This woman Eileen. You're probably right in your conjecture. He'd be quite capable of it."

Paula thought it safer to make no comment.

"He ought to be brought to justice," he muttered after a little further thought. "He's had enough money out of me too. But some people's greed has no limits. You'd better leave this with me now." He got up and walked towards the door. "You've done some good work. I shan't forget it. I'm sorry you won't be able to work on the O'Grady book, but I'm quite serious about the Mountsey job. Send me back the contract and we'll alter it."

He opened the door and shouted. "Jackie! Pete!"

Two minions came running, one from upstairs, one from down.

"Take Dr. Glenning to the stock-room," he said to the girl, "and let her choose some books."

And to the boy: "Come on in, Pete. I've got a job for you. Top priority."

Paula, feeling slightly dazed, followed a tall, fair girl to a large room at the back of the building on the ground floor. Recent publications of the firm, including her own book, were stacked on shelves and lying in piles on a long trestle-table. The sight of a lot of books, old or new, in library, shop, or private house, always brought her a little lift of the heart, an urge to explore and discover new regions of the mind. Normally she would have been delighted to be let loose in such a place, but today she was full of caution and suspicion.

"Does Mr. Bruce really mean I am to help myself?" she asked the girl.

"I don't know," was the reply. "Sometimes he tells you to do something and then you get blamed for doing it."

"Then I think we'd better forget about it," said Paula. "Have you been working here for long?"

"Six months."

"Do you like it?"

"Oh yes. I've always wanted to get into publishing."

"What's your job?"

Jackie, who could not have been older than sixteen, explained in some detail. She helped Mr. Barnard look after the stock-room, she took the mail round to the different offices, she did the photocopying, went on the reception desk when Mrs. Lees was away, and so on and so on. The list seemed endless, and Paula, wondering at first why Jackie should be so content to be everybody's errand girl, ended by thinking that it might, after all, be a good way to learn a lot about the business and the people who worked in it.

"How do you get on with Mr. Bruce?" she asked.

"I get on okay," said the girl. "I do what he tells me if I think he really means it, and if I don't think so, then I wait and see."

"And what happens if you've misjudged?" asked Paula smiling.

"Then he yells at me. But I don't care. It means nothing."

"Is it like that with all the staff?" asked Paula.

"More or less. If you get used to it, you stay and you get on in the firm. And if you don't get used to it, then you leave or you get the sack."

"What an extraordinary way to run a business," said Paula, and Jackie immediately jumped to George's defense. He was a genius. He'd built up the business single-handed. Well no, not exactly single-handed. There'd been others at first. It was a group of former Air Force officers, just after the end of the war. They'd started the business, but George was the force behind it. Paula asked further questions, but Jackie didn't know much more. George Bruce was a genius, and therefore to be forgiven everything. They kept coming back to that.

And he's got the madness of genius, added Paula to herself as she said goodbye to Jackie and to Mrs. Lees at the reception desk. The latter looked a sensible woman, and Paula longed to question her, but she was much too busy with the switchboard. There was, however, another source of information not far away. Now that the object of the investigation was the real George Bruce and not the mythical Rosie O'Grady, the whole scene had shifted completely.

— 17 —

The offices of Broadways Literary Agency were similar to those of George Bruce, but more modest, and while the publishing house had the feeling of exploding with life, the agency felt half-asleep. William Broadway was on holiday, a languid-looking girl told Paula, and his secretary was out at lunch. Oh no, she wasn't; she was just coming downstairs now.

"Somebody to see you, Fran," said the girl, and returned to her study of a travel agency's brochure.

Frances Merivale greeted Paula warmly and inquired about the O'Grady researches.

"They've reached a rather critical point," said Paula, "and there's something I rather urgently want to ask you. But you were just going out."

"I was only going to eat sandwiches by the lake in St. James's Park," said Frances. "It can wait."

"Would you mind if I joined you?"

"Delighted."

They walked across the grass together, skirting the massed ranks of tourists staring, as if hypnotized, at the facade of Buckingham Palace, where nothing was happening at all, and found a place near the café in the park, where a long line of people was waiting to be served.

Paula offered to join the queue.

"Tell me what it is you wanted to ask me," said Frances, "and I'll be thinking about it while I'm waiting."

"I'd like to know anything you can tell me about George

129

Bruce. The start of the business. Who were his original partners, who helped him, what became of them. Absolutely anything you know.''

"It won't be very much, but I'll do my best," promised
Frances.

In fact, it turned out to be more than Paula had hoped for.
William Broadway's secretary had worked for him for years
and was obviously the mainstay of the firm. "It used to be
the best literary agency in London," she said, and mentioned
some famous names that Broadway's father had launched,
"but it's rapidly declining now. I'm only hanging on another
few years for my retirement pension."

"Did Broadway have any special connections with George
Bruce?" asked Paula. "Any special personal link, I mean,
apart from the professional relationship?"

"I've been trying to remember" was the reply. "I don't
think so. Broadways were frightfully gentlemanly and old-
fashioned, and Bruce was full of new ideas. He got going
just after the war and shot up to the top in a matter of years.
The archetypal whiz-kid."

Paula put further questions. Frances seemed glad to talk.
Her memory was good and she had a wide knowledge of the
London publishing scene. She was wasted, thought Paula,
just propping up an ailing business.

George Bruce, as Paula had already learned, was the moving spirit of a little group of RAF men who had spent their
demobilization money on this publishing venture, working at
first from a couple of attic rooms in Soho, and printing the
sort of thing that was thought very daring at that time.

Who were his partners?

Frances did not know their names, but yes, she thought it
very likely that Robin Key was among them at the very beginning. She had never met him personally, but she had had
quite a lot of telephone conversations and correspondence
with him over the years, and had formed the impression that
he knew George Bruce very well.

It was rather absurd, she added, that the O'Grady novels
should come to Broadways Agency at all and not go straight
to the publisher, because Broadway did very little except hand
them over and collect the commission. And arrange for trans-

lation and other rights, of course, but it was very little work in comparison with the income they derived from this author.

Frances had often wondered why Robin Key, acting for Rosie O'Grady, had troubled about an agent at all and had not dealt direct with the publisher. Pressed by Paula, she tried to find a reason for it, and could only suppose that Robin Key had for some reason or other not wanted to have personal dealings with George and was glad of the intermediary. Some people, she added, did prefer to have a buffer between themselves and George.

Paula said she could understand this very well, and for a little while the two women remained silent, drinking their orange juice and looking across at the ever-changing stream of people on the opposite bank of the lake.

"If Robin Key was one of George's early partners," said Paula at last, "I wonder why he broke with him."

"I think George must have quarrelled with most of them," said Frances. "Either he got rid of them when they'd served their purpose, or they got sick of being bullied and cleared out of their own accord. One of them is still on the board of directors, I think, but I doubt if he does anything except collect his money. The other directors are George's cousin, who is an accountant—and they seem to get on all right—and two more who are happy to do what they are told."

"I'm sure Robin would not do as he was told," said Paula, "but if he really was in at the beginning when the going was tough, he must have resented not reaping the rewards later on."

"Presumably he made quite a lot by acting for Rosie O'Grady," commented Frances.

"Yet another middleman," said Paula thoughtfully.

George's remark "He's had a lot out of it" came to her mind, together with a little streak of memory, an illuminating but elusive little streak that she couldn't quite catch hold of.

Then suddenly it came. Robin's own words, during their first visit to High Beechwoods. He had spoken of George not with fear and resentment, but with confidence, almost with triumph, as if he had some sort of hold over him. Both Paula and James had noticed it at the time, but later events had driven it out of their heads.

Blackmail. Robin Key knew something about George.

That made plenty of sense. No wonder George had been so inactive over the disappearance of Joan and so lukewarm in his attempts to uncover the Mystery Lady. And his last attempt, to free himself via Paula, had been very half-hearted. He must have longed to find out something about Robin that would redress the balance, but at the same time he must have been afraid of going too far.

So Paula's suggestion that Robin could have been guilty of some serious crime had given George fresh hope. No wonder he had been in such an extraordinary mood this morning.

"I'll have to get back to the office," said Frances, getting up and brushing the grass from her skirt.

"I'll walk with you," said Paula.

On the way she said, "I'm sorry I can't tell you what this is all about, although I expect you can make a guess. Later on, if it all slots into place and I feel free to talk, I'd like to explain. If you'd like to hear."

Frances said she would very much like to hear. "And by the way," she added, "if you ever feel that you yourself would like to have some sort of a buffer state between yourself and George, we should be very pleased to act as one. I may have rather given the impression that Broadways is on its last legs, but that's not quite true. It's never going to be able to compete with the energetic newcomers, but it's perfectly capable of looking after the interests of an author such as yourself."

"That's a bargain." Paula held out her hand. "I like your way of doing business, Frances. And as far as I'm concerned, you can start looking after me right away. What on earth do I do about this contract I've signed to write this book that can't be published even if it ever gets written? And what about the Charles Mountsey project? That's something I'd really like to do, but if it's going to get me into the sort of mess I seem to be in at present—"

"I think you'd better come back to the office with me now," said Frances, "and we'll see what we can do."

When Paula got home later that afternoon, she called James's number and was disappointed to get no reply. There was so much to tell him. Frances Merivale, during the course of their further discussion, had recollected a former acquaintance of hers who had done some temporary work for George Bruce years ago. After a lot of telephoning they had succeeded in tracking this lady down to the retirement home where she was now living, and her recollections proved to be very interesting indeed.

Yes, Robin Key had certainly been one of George's original colleagues. She remembered him well. She herself had been an inefficient typist and he had been very patient with her. They used to have little chats about photography. She was very much an amateur, but he was first-class. She believed that had been his job in the RAF. No, she had never seen or heard of him again. Somebody had told her that he left the firm soon after her own short spell of work there came to an end.

"Robin Key—expert photographer," typed Paula at the bottom of her copy of the report to George Bruce. "That raises very interesting possibilities. This lady also remembered that in the early days the firm published a lot of risky (presumably near-pornographic) stuff, and some of the staff didn't like it. Even more important, some of the people who put money into the business didn't like it, including George's father, a wealthy but very strait-laced old gentleman.

"Luckily for George and for the publishing business, he died at about this time—drowned in a boating accident.

"The 'luckily' is my own insertion," continued Paula. "Frances Merivale's old acquaintance didn't make any connections or suggest that there was anything suspicious about old Mr. Bruce's death. I am making the connections myself.

"The business was in its infancy. It badly needed money. George's father had money, but George's father disapproved of the firm's publications. George's father had a fatal accident and the firm flourished. And at about this time Robin Key left the firm, but continued to draw money from it, even while he was doing other jobs. Later, when he had taken Rosie O'Grady under his wing, he was paid in the form of excessive royalties on her books."

Paula pulled out the sheet of paper from the typewriter and spoke aloud.

"Well, James, I don't know what your comment on this is going to be, but I'd guess it is much the same as my own."

Surely James must be home by now. Rosie the Fourth would be wanting her supper, and he would never let her go hungry.

But at half past eight there was still no reply, and Paula decided to drive round to his apartment. The possession of her own car was still enough of a novelty to tempt her out on such little excursions. Maybe he was watching television and not answering the phone; or maybe he was out in the garden trying to get the cat to come in.

Paula parked the mini in a leafy side-street a few yards away from the apartment block and walked round to the garden side. There was no sign of a black cat, nor any sign of James, but there was a light on in his kitchen. It was a dull evening, and in any case that room did not get much natural light. Probably he had just got home.

She returned to the main entrance, rang the bell, and put her ear to the intercom. A woman's voice, sounding faint and cracked through the never very efficient mechanism, spoke.

"Who is that, please?"

Paula's first thought was that James had acquired a new girl-friend, and she was conscious of an extraordinary mixture of relief and disappointment. The conflicting emotions were so closely intertwined that it was impossible to disentangle them or to determine which was predominant.

"Who is it?" repeated the voice.

Paula gave her name, and heard the click of the lock on the main door being released. There were four apartments on the ground floor. The one on the left at the back was James's. Curiosity, even a little apprehension, joined with Paula's mix of feelings as she walked across the thick carpet in the hall.

The door of the apartment was ajar.

"May I come in?" called Paula.

The door was pulled wide open.

"I cannot tell you how glad I am to see you," said Joan Cook.

— 18 —

"James didn't want me to phone you," said Joan, after Paula had recovered from her surprise and they were seated side by side on the settee, with Rosie, sprawled between them, receiving a great deal of stroking. "And he didn't want me to answer the phone if it rang. Not because it might be you," she hastily added. "He was hanging about all afternoon hoping to hear from you."

"And I've been calling all evening," said Paula. "Where's he gone, Joan? When is he coming back? And what are you doing here? We were afraid you were"—and her voice became very faint—"dead," she concluded, and to her own astonishment burst into tears.

Joan Cook, seemingly as calm and unmoved as ever, waited in silence for Paula to recover.

"Yes, James told me," she said. "I was rather afraid you might think that, and I hated leaving that letter for you. But the only way to clear this business up was to appear to go along with Robin. The other thing that worried me was this." She lifted the cat onto her lap. "I was so afraid she might be hiding somewhere in the house, but I couldn't find her and I dared not keep Robin waiting any longer. I called him immediately after you left that evening, and he drove down straight away."

"Where from?" interrupted Paula.

"He's got a service flat in Chelsea, and stays there when he's in England."

"You mean he's been living in London?"

"Yes. Why should you be surprised? Robin hasn't been leading a double life, though he does keep right away from George, and indeed from anybody at all connected with publishing."

"Sorry," said Paula, "it's just that I rather thought—"

"—that he might have good reason to hide? Yes, I rather thought so too after your visit to High Beechwoods. But I'd better tell you in the proper order. I'll be as quick as possible.

"When he got to Forest Brook that night he was very exhausted and in a shocking state of nerves. Hardly surprising after all that driving and worrying about you and your researches. He's no longer young. I tried to reassure him, and after a while he calmed down a little and suggested that we should clear out at once. Whatever the outcome of your investigations, or rather, of George's investigations using you as agent, it was plain that a show-house for Rosie O'Grady would not be necessary any more. I thought it was wise to humour him. I really was afraid that he could have a heart attack or some other form of seizure. I drove him up to London—he was quite unfit to drive—and stayed with him in his flat the next two days until he had recovered a little.

"Then we had our heart-to-heart talk. Rosie—Eileen Rosamund—didn't die of consumption in a Swiss sanatorium. She died at High Beechwoods of an overdose of drink and drugs. She was an alcoholic and a manic-depressive. Why did he conceal her death? Because he wanted the books to go on. They were making a lot of money. Even more than they should have done. He was blackmailing George Bruce. Did you know that?"

"I found it out today," said Paula.

"I had no suspicion," went on Joan, "but Robin was frightened enough to tell me the truth. He really thought he was going to die, those days I looked after him in Chelsea. The only thing I couldn't get him to tell me was what his hold over George was."

"I think I can guess," said Paula, and quickly explained her own suspicions.

Joan was sufficiently interested to be diverted from her story.

"I knew that George had put a lot of money into the firm," she said, "and I knew his parents were both dead. I'd always supposed that the money was his wife's, although they've lived apart for years and she has nothing to do with the business. However, let me finish. As soon as Robin was better I told him I was going home. He wanted me to come with him to the Canary Islands, where he's got an apartment, but I told him I'd had enough of hiding and running away. I promised him that I wouldn't tell anybody what he had told me, except you and James. He didn't like that at all, but there was nothing he could do. Robin's no killer, Paula. He's a cheat and probably a blackmailer, but he has got some redeeming qualities. You look sceptical, but remember, I have worked with him for many years.''

''And what did you do then?'' asked Paula.

''I meant to go home—to my cottage near Maidstone. You must visit me there. We'll have our postponed tea-party. But first of all I drove to Forest Brook. I know it sounds silly, but all the time I was looking after Robin I was worrying about the cat.''

''And you found that the letter to me was gone and that somebody had forced open the back door,'' said Paula, ''and you knew it was James and me snooping again.''

''I did indeed, and I then began to worry about *you*. What on earth were you going to do next? Were you yourself going to run into some danger? I drove home to relax and recover, because by this time I too was very tired. After a night's rest I decided to telephone you. That was this morning.''

''I was at George Bruce's office all morning,'' said Paula.

''Yes. When I got no reply from your number, I called James. Luckily he was here, and when I said I very much wanted to see you both, he suggested I should come here. I didn't want to come back to London at all. I dislike it, and I've always got a stupid fear that I might meet somebody from my former life—which is idiotic when you think of London's millions and the fact that I myself have changed out of all recognition in the last thirty years. However, I agreed because it seemed the quickest way to get to see you. If you hadn't arrived just then I should have called your number and not waited any longer for James.''

''But where has he gone?''

''I wish I knew. I told him all I've just told you, and he

said it fitted in with something he'd found out via someone at the BCC.''

''Ah, I see,'' exclaimed Paula, and explained about Caroline.

''Then he'll have gone in search of Robin. Or George,'' said Joan. ''He's determined to be in at the finish, if that's what there is going to be. I like it even less, now that I've spoken to you. Paula, is he capable of impulsive quixotic gestures like trying to save Robin's life if he believed it to be threatened?''

''I thought I knew James,'' Paula replied, ''but he keeps surprising me. Like when he suddenly decided to adopt the cat. Yes, I suppose he is capable of thinking he can do some sort of James Bond act all on his own. I don't like it either. Not a bit.''

''Then we must do something too,'' said Joan firmly. ''We can't just sit here.''

They sat in silence for a moment.

''High Beechwoods,'' said Paula suddenly.

''Why?''

''Lonely, isolated, deserted.''

''That might suit George, if he is out to dispose of Robin,'' said Joan, ''but I can't imagine Robin ever going there again in any circumstances, let alone late at night with his blackmail victim.''

''Not alone,'' said Paula, ''but if James were with him—''

They stared at each other.

''No,'' said Joan at last. ''Nothing would get Robin to go back there. He hates the place. No. They'll be at Robin's London apartment and not answering the phone. So we'd better go there. If we get no reply, the caretaker may be able to help.''

''It doesn't sound the sort of place for a confrontation,'' said Paula, ''but I suppose we'd better go there first. What about Rosie? Does James let her out?''

''No. She's got a tray. And we'd better leave a note for James in case he gets back before we do.''

''And another for his cleaning woman to find in the morning in case George shoots the lot of us and none of us gets back at all,'' said Paula lightly.

But Joan did not smile. ''I think that would be a good

idea," she said, and Paula, who had been trying to comfort herself by putting the whole business back into the realm of intellectual inquiry, felt again all the immediacy of intense apprehension.

Joan suggested that she should drive to Chelsea; it would be quicker because she knew the way.

When they were nearly there, she said, "If George really is as crazy as you think, I shall blame myself if there has been any tragedy. I didn't take James seriously enough. And I should have done."

"You didn't know," said Paula. "You didn't realize just how desperate George was. If you had seen him this morning—"

Paula was scanning the quiet side-street as she spoke. On the right were gardens, surrounded by iron railings. On the left was a terrace of eighteenth-century houses, with white paintwork and with a profusion of flowering plants on the broad low doorsteps.

"There's his car!" cried Paula.

Joan drew in behind the white Rover. "Robin's will be in the garage. You don't know what George drives, I suppose?"

"Sorry."

The doorbells were to the left of the door. There were no name-plates alongside.

"Number 3," said Joan.

There was no response.

"There must be someone there," whispered Paula.

Joan tried again, holding her finger for a long time on the bell.

At last they heard a man's voice, sounding very faint.

"Who is that, please?"

"Robin, it's Joan. Paula Glenning is with me. We thought James Goff might have come to see you, and since his car is here—Robin! What's the matter? Aren't you going to let us in? Robin!"

There was no further sound. The two women looked at each other in alarm. Then Paula said, "Someone's opened the door. Come on."

She was inside and halfway up the first flight of stairs before the slower-moving Joan had reached the bottom and called out that there was a lift.

Paula did not hear. Joan rang for the elevator and they reached the door of apartment number 3 at the same moment.

It was opened by James. Paula called his name but he said nothing. He stepped aside to let them enter and then closed the door behind them all.

"James," said Paula again, "what on earth—"

"I'll do the explaining," said a new voice. "Sit there, Joan. Don't move. Come here, Paula."

Paula thought she had been prepared for anything, but now that it came to the point she found it impossible to believe. This could not be happening, it could not be true that George Bruce had grabbed hold of her and was pointing a deadly looking little weapon at her and saying, "This is my hostage. This makes it much easier. Nobody wants any harm to come to Paula. Do you?"

Nobody replied.

This is not true, said Paula to herself over and over again; in a minute I am going to wake up.

— 19 —

"Don't worry, girl," said George to Paula in a ghastly imitation of his earlier genial manner. "I don't want anybody to get hurt and the sooner this business is settled, the better for us all. Robin has the negatives of some photographs that I particularly want to get hold of. I had hoped that your researches would help me, but unfortunately he is being extremely obstinate about it. I told him what you said in your report and I thought we could come to an amicable agreement, but he refuses to meet me. Hence the recourse to more desperate measures."

He let go of Paula's arm but kept her covered.

"May I sit down, please?" she asked.

"Certainly, my dear. Just there. I'll stand behind you. I'm sure it won't be for long. Wiser counsels will soon prevail and we can all go home. Where are those negatives, Robin?"

"They aren't here. I told you. They aren't in this apartment."

Robin Key was leaning back in a deep armchair, looking white and ill. Joan, who had been ordered to take the chair next to him, looked at him in concern. Only James remained standing, just inside the door, and looking, to Paula's horror, very much as if he was considering the possibility of making a rush at George.

"Then where are they?" asked George.

"I don't know," muttered Robin.

"I don't believe you. Oh, come on now," continued George as Robin did not respond. "There's a good fellow.

You've had your fun. And your money too. Nobody's going to take that away from you. Why don't you finish with it now? What's the sense in going on like this? I don't wish you any harm. I don't wish anybody any harm, as I keep telling you. Give me those negatives now and then we can forget all about it.''

''They aren't here,'' said Robin.

''But you've just said you didn't know where they were. If you know they aren't here, then you must know where they are.''

It seemed to Paula, relieved now that she could no longer actually see her danger, that there was a change for the worse in his manner of speaking. She had stopped telling herself that this was not happening and was beginning to assess her chances of coming alive out of this luxuriously furnished room. So long as George retained a trace of his bullying, genial personality, she believed her chances were good, but if there was one of those sudden changes of mood, of which she knew he was capable—

She longed to ask the others to humour him, to pretend to go along with him and find some way of tricking him, but knew that she must not speak. It seemed to her that Robin was genuinely in a state of shock. After all, according to Joan, he had been quite seriously ill. And James, glowering at George, was not helping at all; and the cool, calm Joan, her chief hope, was now making it even worse.

''It's not good shouting at him, George,'' she said. ''He isn't well. He's only just getting over a heart attack, and if you're not careful he'll have another and you'll never learn where your photographs are.''

''Oh,'' he said with a feeble attempt at a sneer, ''you wouldn't tell me? Wild horses wouldn't drag it from you? Spoken like a true O'Grady heroine.''

''I said nothing at all,'' replied Joan. ''I haven't the slightest idea what photographs you are talking about, but if you want them so badly, then I would think your best plan is to put down that repulsive-looking weapon and ask Robin's help in a civilized manner. In any case, it's probably all bluff,'' she added to the room at large.

''It's not bluff.'' Robin roused himself to turn to Joan. ''It's loaded.''

"Then in that case you'd better give him the pictures. Where are they, Robin?"

There was a silence. At last Robin said, "At High Beechwoods."

Paula uttered a little sound and leaned forward.

"Sit still," came the voice from just behind her, and she leaned back again and closed her eyes, feeling suddenly very weak as she realized what was going to happen next.

"Where at High Beechwoods?" asked George.

"In the Spanish hardback editions of the first four novels," said Robin in a barely audible voice. "Stuck to the inside of the back flap of the book jacket."

"Give me the key," said George, and Robin felt in a pocket and handed it over.

"Okay," said George. "Come on, Paula."

In the doorway he addressed the three people left in the room.

"They'd better be there. You know what will happen to Paula if they aren't. Or if you call the police."

On the way downstairs Paula wondered whether to scream for help or to try and escape. Surely George would not shoot, not here in this house with other people around. At the front door she was particularly tempted, but in the end she decided that he was mad enough for anything and that it was safer to go along.

Thus one part of her mind was reasoning, while yet another part of her mind was noting, with some surprise, that it was not possible to keep at a high pitch of fear; that fear had peaked and was now, temporarily, at least, in descent, and that she was actually beginning to feel an almost detached curiosity as to what would happen next.

In the room upstairs Joan and James spoke quickly.

"Police?"

"Too risky. I'll follow myself."

Robin, deathly pale, gave a little moan.

"I'll have to stay with him," said Joan. "Good luck, James."

But he had already gone.

From the doorway he watched the progress of George's car towards the corner of the main road. A little blue Vauxhall,

good for London traffic but not so good for motorways. It
was taking a slow and wavering course along the quiet road.
James, awaiting the right moment to follow, was puzzled.
What was George doing? Was he drunk?

And then it dawned on him. Of course. Paula was driving.
Under threat, in true classic style. No wonder she was me-
andering about, in a strange car, in such circumstances.

Unless, of course, she was doing it on purpose, deliberately pretending that she could not cope with the car.

Then what does she want me to do? James asked himself.
It would not be difficult to stage a smash that would immo-
bilize them all and attract public attention. Nobody need be
seriously hurt, except perhaps Paula, who would probably be
shot dead.

No. Paula would not want any drastic action unless there
was absolutely no alternative. From his own short acquaintance with George, James felt that she was right in thinking
he was quite unpredictable.

So for the time being, it would be best just to follow.

The driver of George's car had either accustomed herself
to the controls or had received a sharp warning. The mean-
dering stopped, and the car moved smartly up to the corner
and turned left.

James drove to the corner, waited for a bus to go by, and
then turned left too. Now he had a new problem to worry
about. Paula might guess that he would follow, but which
would make it easier for her: to know for sure or not to know
for sure? She would be looking in the driving mirror. It would
be easy enough to come into view and then drop back again.
George, even if he was looking back, would not recognize
the car.

Lambeth Bridge? No. Then they must be crossing the river
at Westminster.

James was not aware that he was talking aloud to himself.
His whole consciousness had settled down into three strands
of thought, separate but closely interwoven. The first was
concerned with watching the road and keeping George's car
in sight; the second, much less straightforward, was concerned with what he himself was proposing to do at the end
of the journey; and the third, most complicated of all, was
his attempt to enter into Paula's thoughts and feelings, to live

through the horror of the situation with her and, somehow or other, in so doing, to give her strength.

That the journey could end in disaster he refused even to admit. Every time there seemed any danger of such a thought leaking into his mind he deliberately began to picture to himself the last stages of the journey and to consider at which part of the road it would be best to engineer some sort of crash, if that was what he finally decided to do.

After the first few nightmarish minutes, Paula found that it was not, after all, so difficult to forget about the reason for the journey and to concentrate on the driving. In fact, there was very little else that she could do. The Vauxhall was completely strange to her and she had to ask George where the switch for the headlamps was, and how to work the screen-wipers, for it had begun to rain. His replies were short, but not particularly angry or impatient. Rather like a driving instructor.

This thought produced in Paula a nervous giggle, which she instantly suppressed. When she was driving with more confidence she decided to try a friendly comment, having remembered that one method of coping with hostage-taking was to get into some sort of personal relationship with the hijacker.

"I like this car," she said. "I rather wish I'd bought one instead of a mini."

The remark was not a success. He said nothing, but she could sense an increase in the tension.

Okay then. Leave that idea alone. How about trying to think what the others would do? Robin would do nothing. Perhaps he had already had another attack. And Joan would stay with him. Her loyalty to him seemed unshakable.

What about James? No prizes, Paula said to herself, for guessing what James would do. In fact, during those first awful moments when her hands were shaking so much that George's car had wandered all over the road, she had had no clear thoughts at all except a longing to see the familiar white Rover in the mirror.

She had not seen it until half an hour later, and then only for a second.

Again she nearly laughed, this time in relief. At least James has had some recent practice in car-chasing, she said to her-self. And he wouldn't do anything crazy, like trying to run them into the hedge when they got out into the country roads. The best thing, her mind addressed James, is to keep going until we reach High Beechwoods; don't let George know you are there, but be sure you get to the house quickly, before he has time to find that the negatives are not tucked away in those Spanish editions of the early novels.

For surely they could not be there. Robin had made up that story to save his own skin and maintain his hold over George. By the time they got back to London, if indeed they ever did get back to London, Robin would have flown, literally, to his semi-tropical haven, taking his pictures with him. And prob-ably Joan would have gone too.

If you had been blackmailing somebody for years you would never, even under threat, tell them where the incrim-inating material was unless there was absolutely no alterna-tive. In any case you would certainly not leave it in an abandoned house, where anybody could easily get in.

Or would you? Perhaps after all that was not such a bad hiding-place. Nobody was likely to come near the house. The village was obviously completely incurious, and it was too modest a dwelling to attract the attention of housebreakers. Anyone coming across it during a long country walk might wonder at its isolation, but the only people likely to enter would be homeless or fugitive, seeking shelter.

"Look out!" yelled George.

He sounded both furious and terrified. Paula had been so absorbed in her train of thought that she was not concentrat-ing on her driving. The big car coming the other way and doing a dangerous piece of overtaking missed them by inches.

George obviously thought she had purposely failed to brake and was deliberately seeking an accident.

"I'm sorry," said Paula. "I'm not used to night driving."

She had to say something and this seemed a harmless re-mark. He said no more but she felt that the tension in him was greater than ever. If he doesn't find those negatives he won't know what to do with me, she thought, and if he does find them he won't know what to do with me either. It's not good shooting me and leaving me in the house because ev-erybody will know he is guilty. And he won't want to take me with him, wherever he's going, because I'll become more and more of a nuisance. He didn't think it through; he just saw an immediate use for a hostage.

This was a comforting train of thought as they approached Forest Brook. Paula decided that George was not going to shoot her, whatever happened. But almost immediately it occurred to her that she was using her reason, or as much of it as she could summon up in the circumstances, whereas George was beyond all reason.

And where was James? All the way through the darkened village, over the little bridge and up the hill, Paula had been hoping to see the lights of a car behind them, but there were none. The night was dark, the rain had settled into a steady drizzle, and there seemed to be nobody in the whole world except herself and this crazy gunman.

Perhaps James had had an accident; perhaps he had been caught by a speed cop; perhaps he had missed the turning, as he had on the very first time they ever came here.

Paula turned George's car into the track. The wheels skidded on the wet grass and made progress very difficult. The only comforting thought she could now summon up was that George was going to find it physically difficult to keep the weapon pointing at her while he was actually hunting for the pictures. But even that comfort deserted her after a moment's reflection, because of course he wouldn't hunt for the pictures: She would be doing that herself.

20

Paula slipped on the wet grass as she got out of the car and nearly fell. Again it was unintentional, but every single movement she made now would be interpreted as an attempt to escape. If she were to make a serious effort, he would shoot. She had no doubt of that now. He didn't know what to do; he was as terrified and desperate as she was herself.

The lights of the car, which he had told her to leave on, showed up the garden and the ghostly trunks of the beech trees beyond the hedge. Like a stage set, lit up by the footlights. Paula's mind seemed to detach itself from her body and wander among the beech trees, observing the damp earth and the fallen leaves and twigs, and listening for the rustling sounds of night creatures—an owl, a fox.

A puppet figure, which she seemed to be operating by remote control, moved towards the door of the house and put the key into the lock and turned it.

And then the puppet and the wandering mind came together in a great sense of shock as she fell full-length on the floor. And lying there, half-stunned, she heard the sound of the long-expected shot, then shouting, then the noise of a car engine, then silence.

After what seemed a long while she sat up, twisted around a little, and decided that she was bruised but not seriously hurt. She had not the slightest idea what had happened, but it looked as if George had fired a shot and then gone. No point in wondering why. She must get out of here, and it was going to be difficult because it was so dark. The outline of

148

the open door was very dimly visible but there were no more car headlamps for guidance.

The farm. Or the village. Farther to walk, but more choice of people to ask for help.

Paula got to her feet. She felt weak and ill and her right leg hurt quite badly, but she would get there somehow, even if in the end she had to crawl. The sense of acting of her own free will was like a healing drink.

She came out of the front door, stood for a moment trying to get her bearings in the darkness, and then suddenly remembered the photographs. Had George found what he came for? Had she been lying semi-conscious for a long time?

The sense of freedom of action was so exhilarating that in spite of her aching weakness she felt a longing to know whether the pictures were there.

If she had had a light, she would have stopped to look, but in the dark it was pointless. And there was also no sense in fumbling about trying to find the main electricity switch. Curiosity must wait. The top priority now was to look after herself.

She moved very cautiously down from the low doorstep onto the garden path and then stopped again, struck with a primitive panic that was worse than any of the fears she had suffered that evening.

Somebody was coming towards her along the garden path. She could feel and hear more than she could see.

This was true nightmare. Paralysis. Inability even to scream. And, as in a dream, it seemed to go on for a very long time before she heard a very familiar voice.

"Paula—are you all right? I'm sorry I had to trip you up. And he's got away, damn him."

Paula drew a deep breath, then said, "Have you got a flashlight, James?"

"Yes, only the battery's getting low."

' Will it last to inspect the books? Or have you already looked?"

"Of course I haven't looked. I've been otherwise engaged."

"Yes, I know. Tell me later. But let's look at those books now. Please, James."

"You are quite unbelievable," he grumbled as he helped

her into the living-room. "Kidnapped, snatched from the jaws
of death, leg broken, and all you can think of is those bloody
books."

"I haven't got a broken leg. It's horribly bruised." Paula
felt for an armchair and collapsed into it. "Do hurry up,
James. I'm dying to ask what happened, but I must know this
first."

He was searching along the shelves. The flashlight certainly did seem to be rather faint.

"Here you are," he said at last, dropping a couple of vol-
umes into her lap. "Look for yourself."

Paula looked. "There's nothing here," she said, "and no
sign that there ever has been anything concealed here. Let's
see the next two."

James fetched them. The same result.

"What about the other Spanish editions?" said Paula.

At this point James went on strike.

"What about the Italian?" he shouted. "And the French
and the German and the Russian and the Japanese and all the
rest of the suppurating trash! Don't you care that you could
be dead? If that's all you care, then I've a bloody good mind
to leave you here."

And in a fury he kicked at the books that Paula had let fall
to the floor, and dropped the flashlight, which instantly went
out altogether.

"I'm sorry," said Paula very meekly, but instantly spoilt
the effect of her words by beginning to laugh.

After a moment's hesitation, James laughed too.

"I'll fetch the car," he said. "I left it in the place where
we hid before. Won't be long."

But Paula stood up. "I'm coming with you."

"You won't enjoy walking along that cart-track in the
dark."

"I thought I was going to have to walk all the way to the
village," she retorted. "If you're going to fall into a ditch
and break your ankle, I'd rather know about it than sit here
worrying."

"All right then. We'll stagger along together."

It was indeed a dark and dismal way, wet, too, and becoming very misty. Paula climbed into the white Rover with a

feeling of immense relief, and, in the comfort of its light and warmth, examined her bruises.

"I'm awfully sorry," said James. "I'm afraid that was my fault. You see, I'd found this hammer and I was going to use it on George while he was opening the door. I'd realized that would be his most vulnerable moment. But when I looked through the window and saw that you were going to come in first—well, the only thing to do was trip you up as you stepped in and get you out of the way while I went for George. You weren't meant to get a Rugby tackle, but I was rather nervous. Anyway, it did work. Up to a point."

"Up to a point! It worked superbly!" Paula flung her arms round his neck and then immediately sank back into her own seat and said, "Look, if I once give way I shall collapse completely. What do you want to do now?"

"Get you home quickly."

"And George?"

"Silly of me to try to catch him," said James as he started the engine. "I hit him on the shoulder of the arm that was holding the gun, but he still managed to fire. It all happened more or less simultaneously—you falling and me hitting him and him shooting. I don't know whether he thought he'd hit you or whether he just panicked or what happened. Anyway, he ran. I did just wait to check that you weren't badly hurt before I went after him, and of course by that time he'd backed his car halfway down the track. It was infuriating to let him get away, and I did wonder whether I'd a chance of getting to the Rover in time to follow him but of course there wasn't a hope."

"Quite apart from leaving me lying on the floor," said Paula.

"Exactly."

As they passed through the village, Paula said, "This is a lot more pleasant than trying to wake someone up and persuading them to let me use the phone."

And a little later she said, "When did you decide to take another route and get to the house first?"

James thought it was when they were about halfway there. "I had to come a long way round," he added. "I had to hurry."

"It must have been hair-raising," said Paula. "I'm glad I wasn't with you."

"And your journey wasn't hair-raising?"

"Oddly enough," replied Paula quite seriously, "it wasn't as terrifying as one might expect. It was rather interesting. And comforting, in a way, to know how one actually does react in such drastic circumstances. What do you think will happen to George?"

"God knows."

"Will he go back to Robin's place?"

"They won't let him in if he does. And now you're safe, they could call the police."

"But they don't know I'm safe," said Paula, suddenly agitated. "Ought we to stop and telephone?"

"No," said James very definitely. "It can wait till we've got home and had a wash and drunk gallons of whiskey or tea or whatever else we need."

It turned out to be large bowls of hot soup, followed by coffee and cigarettes. When they were both feeling stronger and less tense, and Rosie the Fourth had been given a second dinner, James suggested they should call Robin's flat.

"It's two o'clock in the morning," said Paula, yawning.

"I doubt if anybody's gone to sleep," said James.

He let the phone ring for several minutes before giving up. When at last he replaced the receiver he turned round to speak to Paula and saw that she was curled up at the end of the settee, fast asleep. He found a blanket and placed it within her reach, picked up the cat, switched off the living-room light, and closed the door.

Five minutes later he too was fast asleep. Rosie the Fourth, having done little else but sleep for the previous six hours, prodded in vain at James for some time before finally deciding that there was nothing to be done but go to sleep again herself.

James was the first to wake. After feeding Rosie to keep her quiet, and making coffee in order to convince himself that it really was another day, he opened the living-room door very carefully.

Paula had stretched herself out on the settee under the blanket, with cushions under her head. She made no movement. He shut the door again, drank more coffee, and picked up the extension telephone in the bedroom.

Joan's voice answered almost at once. "James? Paula?"

"She's fine. She's asleep at the moment."

"Thank God."

There was a brief silence.

"I tried calling you last night," said James, "but there was no reply."

"I came in very late," said Joan. "Robin was taken to hospital not long after you left. He died about two o'clock this morning. He rallied enough to talk a little. Will you and Paula come over here, James? I ought to tell you what he said, but I don't feel able to come to Hampstead."

"Of course you don't. I'll wake Paula at once. We'll be as quick as we can."

When they got there, they could see at once the change in Joan. She looked not only very tired, but also old, and somehow shrunken.

"I know you have been wondering," she said to Paula, "why I should have concerned myself so much with Robin, apart from the books. It is nothing in the least bit sensational, but it has been extremely important to me. He had known my husband. They were at the same air base for some time. It was a link, you see. Like a little lifeline."

Neither James nor Paula could find anything to say.

"Robin had great abilities," went on Joan, "but he never seemed to be able to concentrate them on any worthwhile purpose of his own. It seemed that he had to have some sort of intrigue, some deception to keep up. And he must have been bitterly resentful of George's success, of his single-minded energy.

"He gained enormous satisfaction from feeling that George was in his power, particularly as it was all a bluff."

"Bluff?" exclaimed James and Paula simultaneously.

"Yes. There were no photographs. Hadn't you guessed?"

"I'd begun to suspect," said Paula.

"He didn't want to tell me," went on Joan, "even when he was dying. But I had worked it out for myself and he had no escape. He was with George and his father on the occasion when their yacht got into difficulties, and as usual he had his camera with him, ever ready. He could actually have taken pictures of George pushing the old man overboard but he didn't. He says that he was not even particularly shocked or surprised. George and his father were both very quick-tempered. In any case, at that time violent death was very much a commonplace. At the inquest he confirmed George's story of the accident, and it was only later that he decided he could have some fun by pretending he had taken photographs.

"George believed him. I would have believed him too. But his fun with George had got him caught in a trap. He could never persuade George that the pictures did not exist. Never. The hardest thing in the world is to prove something's non-existence. And last night the trap closed on Robin."

"And very nearly closed on Paula too," said James with a quiet anger that Paula could only echo in her own heart and mind.

"Yes," said Joan, "I am not trying to excuse him. Now," she went on in a different tone of voice, "I want to hear your story."

She was trying her best to assume an air of interested attention, but it was obvious that she did not really want to hear anything. She was deep in her own weariness and her own lonely memories and was talking to them only from a sense of duty.

James explained as briefly as possible what had happened. Paula said nothing. What was the use of a good story, she was thinking, for the events of last night did make a good story, if there was no audience? The way James was telling it, it was about as interesting as a bus timetable.

"I don't know what can have happened to George," he concluded. "I've no idea where the shot went, and I don't think I can have done him any great harm. At any rate, he wasn't too badly hurt to drive away."

"Oh. Didn't you hear the news?" Joan came out of her lethargy for a moment and looked more like her former self.

"We've been sleeping," replied Paula. "We've heard no news this morning."

"It was on the eight-o'clock bulletin. They found him about a mile away from Forest Brook. He'd crashed the car into a telegraph pole and was killed instantly."

James asked further questions, but Joan knew no more.

Her little burst of animation was over and she was obviously longing for them to go.

"You must come and see me some time," she said at the door. "We must have our much-postponed tea-party."

Paula thanked her, knowing that this event would never take place. Joan had moved away from them into new realms of loneliness.

In the car Paula said, "All those years and all those books, and I suppose all the time she was just surviving on the memory of a few weeks of happiness. Can you understand that, James?"

He shook his head.

"It's terrible. It's such a waste. A sort of substitute life," said Paula.

James did not answer for a while. Then he said, "Perhaps that's true of all fiction writers, good and bad alike. A sort of substitute life."

"And of all biographers too?"

"I wouldn't know. That's the question I should like to put to you. But not today. First things first. Breakfast or brunch. Then I've simply got to write that review."

"And I must call Frances and find out who will be taking over George's job."

"Maybe you can write a book after all," said James. "It'll make a good story, and with Robin and George both dead—"

"But Joan is alive."

They came into James's flat and opened the kitchen door to see Rosie O'Grady the Fourth squeezing in through a narrow gap at the top of the window and dropping, rather clumsily, into the sink.

"At least we aren't going to lose this one," said James, lifting her out.

Paula agreed. "She's real enough, thank goodness. The one and only real Rosie."

While they were eating she said, "I wonder how much Joan really knew. She must have known much more about Robin and George than she admitted."

"But we'll never find out," said James. "There's your true Mystery Lady."

Anna Clarke was born in Cape Town and educated in Montreal and Oxford. She holds degrees in economics and English literature and has held a wide variety of jobs, mostly in publishing and university administration. She is the author of eighteen previous novels, including *Cabin 3033*, *Last Judgement*, *Soon She Must Die*, *We the Bereaved*, and *Letter From the Dead*, published by the Crime Club.